Alyssa McCarthy's Magical Missions:
Book 1

The Frights of Fiji

Sunayna Prasad

Alyssa McCarthy's Magical Missions: Book 1
The Frights of Fiji

© by Sunayna Prasad. All
rights reserved.

Cover Art by Enggar

Adirasa

The Frights of Fiji

Sunayna Prasad

1

The raindrops darkened into black, looking as if ink fell from the sky. Alyssa leaned closer to them. She squinted to determine the shapes they formed on the kitchen window… letters.

No! That couldn't happen. Yet, a message spelled out as more pigments plopped onto the glass. Alyssa gasped at what it said.

Your life will never be the same again, Alyssa McCarthy, as magic will interfere.

What? Magic didn't exist—at least that'd been what others had told her when she was little. No one on Orion Street could possess enchanted abilities.

Alyssa had lived here since she'd lost her parents in that car crash five years ago. She'd only been seven then. How would she tell her uncle, Bruce, about this? He'd consider her crazy. He'd already toughened up his attitude and rules. So he might consider it an excuse to escape this house.

Although Alyssa's parents had designated her godfather as the first priority guardian, Uncle Bruce forbade her to try and contact him. He'd hidden the phone number and other information about him.

Since Alyssa's aunt, Laura, had died three years ago, Uncle Bruce had required fun to be earned. And that took more effort than Alyssa could often accomplish.

Turning around, she spotted her babysitter, Mrs. Hutchinson, examining the kitchen floor. Alyssa's eleven-year-old cousin, Hailey, watched the progress. Hailey had mopped the floor. Would she earn a break now? Ever since her uncle, Bruce, had hired Mrs. Hutchinson, Mrs. Hutchinson had admired the way Hailey had done her chores more than Alyssa.

"Hailey, you can take a break until your next chore," said Mrs. Hutchinson. "Alyssa, get back to work. You've been staring at the rain for too long."

"Okay." Alyssa turned back—only to see the message gone and the rain back to its normal transparency.

"What did I say?" asked Mrs. Hutchinson.

Alyssa sighed. "Fine, I'll finish washing the dishes."

She scrubbed her dish and glass with soap under warm running water. Her eyes focused on just those. No way would she want Mrs. Hutchinson to catch her looking out the window again. Mrs. Hutchinson was only in her sixties, but she'd sometimes seem to forget that was 2010 and not 1960 with her guidelines. Yet, it had taken Alyssa a while to realize that she wouldn't even tolerate the mildest kind of nonsense, such as getting distracted by a windowpane when having to perform chores.

Now that she finished washing her dishes, Alyssa put them to the side and grabbed some paper towels to dry them.

"What do you think you're doing?" Mrs. Hutchinson asked.

Alyssa stopped. "I'm just—"

"The last few times I was here, you left little bits of food on your dishes."

"But they were stuck."

"Let me inspect them. Also, if something is rubbery, you have to wash it again."

"Why?"

"Because clean dishes aren't supposed to be rubbery. And boy, did you do such a sloppy job. Look at that stain on your sweater."

Alyssa looked down.

"That looks like chocolate."

Alyssa blushed and arched her eyebrows. "Hey—it's just water." She covered the stain at the bottom of her sweater's V-neck.

But Mrs. Hutchinson waved her index finger. "Don't you 'hey' me, Alyssa. That's rude. In my days, kids respected their elders. We never would dare talk to them that way unless we didn't mind them smacking our bottoms."

"Things change."

"Not when I'm here, they don't. Now let me do my inspection."

Great—an inspection! How long would Mrs. Hutchinson take? She might spend a couple minutes or maybe twenty. Alyssa crossed her arms and tapped her foot. She wanted her break now. She wished to read, rest, do a small craft, like lanyards—anything but wait for Mrs. Hutchinson to finish her task.

"Mrs. Hutchinson?" Alyssa asked.

"Whatever you need to say, wait till I'm done," she said.

Alyssa sighed. She continued to watch Mrs. Hutchinson run her finger down the middle of the front of the dish. She then rubbed it back and forth. When she put it down and nodded, Alyssa figured out that the dish had nothing on it.

Mrs. Hutchinson spent a few minutes of running her finger down the glass. She put it down and turned to Alyssa. "You're good. Now what did you want to tell me?"

"Um . . . if I tell you, can you not give me a hard time?"

"Okay."

"There was writing on the window."

Mrs. Hutchinson pursed her lips and tilted her head. "Really?"

"Yeah."

"Nonsense."

"No, really, it was there."

"There was nothing there when I came, and there's nothing there right now. So don't tell me stories."

"But it's not a story."

"I don't want to hear any more. Now it's time for your next chore."

"Aw, but I wanted my break."

"Too bad. You have to go vacuum the living room."

Alyssa dragged her feet toward the living room and took the vacuum from the corner. She cleaned and thought about that writing as well as how Mrs. Hutchinson wouldn't believe her. Would a nicer babysitter have believed her? Mrs. Hutchinson had watched her and Hailey for three years, and not once had she smiled or assisted with anything.

After vacuuming the carpet for about five minutes, Alyssa decided that she had tidied the floor enough. So she stopped and put the vacuum away.

"Hailey, you and Alyssa need to go get the mail now!" Mrs. Hutchinson called, facing the staircase.

"Coming!" cried Hailey.

Another rule Uncle Bruce had placed on Alyssa and Hailey was they could only go outside together. He worried about people taking them or something, even though Alyssa would turn thirteen next month. But that rule had been placed because a few months ago, Uncle Bruce had heard about a seventeen-year-old boy who had been shot while skateboarding in his neighborhood. Violence could even happen here in Bursnell, New Jersey.

Hailey and Alyssa headed to the closet and put their raincoats on until Mrs. Hutchinson said, "It stopped raining outside."

"Already?" asked Alyssa.

"Yes." Mrs. Hutchinson went to the bathroom.

The girls walked outside toward the mailbox. Alyssa pulled the mail and headed back toward the door. But mud bubbled from the ground near the house. It piled up, looking like horse manure, and grew as more soil emerged. Alyssa dropped her jaw and stared at it.

"Alyssa, what's going on?" Hailey asked.

"No idea," said Alyssa.

The dirt stopped piling up, but it continued to bubble, and the effects spread throughout the whole pile. The bubbles stopped popping up and down. Alyssa and Hailey gasped as they expanded. They kept their mouths open as the bubbles merged together, each one attached to another, forming a single bigger shape. Alyssa and Hailey stepped back as the now giant bubble swelled. And it . . . *popped!* Particles of exploding mud landed on the girls. They shrieked.

The front door opened to reveal a glowering Mrs. Hutchinson. "What the heck have you two been doing?"

"T-the mud . . . it e-exploded," said Hailey.

"Nonsense!" growled Mrs. Hutchinson. "Get inside!"

The girls returned inside, pulling and wiping the mud out of their hair. Alyssa could spot the mud in her straight pale-blonde tresses, unlike Hailey, who likely needed more patience to search for globs in her elbow-length red locks. But Alyssa's hair fell a few inches past her hips, so cleaning out the mud would take longer, even with the shorter layers in the front.

"How could dirt explode?" Mrs. Hutchinson stomped.

"I-I think it was magic!" exclaimed Alyssa.

"There's no such thing as magic!" screamed Mrs. Hutchinson. "Alyssa, you're twelve years old. You're too old to say things like that!"

"But nothing else can make mud explode!" Alyssa said.

"Mrs. Hutchinson, we swear it did!" whined Hailey.

"Enough!" snapped Mrs. Hutchinson. "You and Hailey—go upstairs and take showers!"

Alyssa followed Hailey up the stairs and heaved a sigh. How else would the mud have splattered all over them? Mrs.

Hutchinson couldn't have thought they'd play in the mud like small children.

"Alyssa, can I shower first?" asked Hailey.

"Sure," said Alyssa.

As Hailey strode into the bathroom, Alyssa walked into her room. She scratched more mud off her skinny jeans (the only jeans she'd worn ever since they'd come into style) and the back of her hand. She stood by her bed since she wanted to keep it clean.

She considered the writing on the window and the exploding mud. Someone wanted magic to interfere with her life, but who, and how come?

Also, why hadn't she ever seen wizardry before? Why would her parents and others tell her that it hadn't existed? Did sorcery just start on earth? Had it hidden somewhere? There had to be some reason why no one had ever believed in it.

Alyssa thought about the possibility that maybe magic might only interfere if she stayed here in her uncle's house. Maybe if her godfather could arrange with his lawyer to let her move in with him, sorcery would hopefully leave her alone. However, unlike science, anything could occur with magic, which meant that it could follow her wherever she went.

The sound produced by the bathroom's running water ended, which let Alyssa know that Hailey had finished. Now she could have a turn.

After about five minutes showering, Alyssa stepped out and headed back to her room. She put on leggings and a long shirt. But she gasped at something appearing out of nowhere on her bed. Now that had to have come from . . . magic.

Approaching it, she saw that it was a folded piece of paper. She opened it and read it.

Hello Alyssa McCarthy,

You must be wondering about the writing on your window, the exploding mud, and the note that appeared here. Who was responsible for them? You'll find out at some point.

Anonymous

Anonymous? How dare someone create incidents and not say his or her name! Alyssa needed to know his or her identity in order to report him or her. She didn't want strange, magical occurrences to keep happening.

Regardless of that, now she had proof to Mrs. Hutchinson that the writing and exploding mud had occurred. Mrs. Hutchinson had seen her write before, and this looked nothing like hers. She handwrote in a half-print and half-script style. This, however, was pure print.

Alyssa jogged down the stairs and carried the note. "Mrs. Hutchinson, I have something to show you."

"Not right now, Alyssa." Mrs. Hutchinson left the kitchen. "You and Hailey have to go wash my car."

"But it's quick."

"You can show me after you're done with my car." Mrs. Hutchinson turned to Hailey, who emptied the dishwasher and put dishes away. "Are you almost done?"

"I think so," said Hailey.

"How many dishes do you have left?" asked Mrs. Hutchinson.

"Uh . . ." Hailey looked at the top rack. "Four."

"Okay, hurry up." Mrs. Hutchinson turned to Alyssa. "Why don't you go put that piece of paper away?"

"But this is what I need to show you."

"Do I have to repeat what I said before?"

"But—"

"Alyssa, do as you're told." Mrs. Hutchinson pointed to the staircase.

Alyssa sighed. This note contained so much crucial information. Only that paper itself had evidence to show that those incidents had occurred.

After putting the note back in her room, Alyssa headed down the stairs and walked with Hailey toward the garage. The two grabbed sponges, buckets, and soap for washing cars. They filled the buckets with water and scrubbed Mrs. Hutchinson's car.

"I wish we had another babysitter," muttered Alyssa.

"What was on the piece of paper?" asked Hailey.

Alyssa told her.

"Who wrote it?"

"There was no name on it. Just 'anonymous.'"

A girl whistling turned Alyssa's attention away from the car. She leaned her head toward the sidewalk and saw her friend from grade school, Madison Jennings, riding her scooter.

"Hi, Alyssa," said Madison. The wind blew her long dark-brown waves across her face. She stopped at Alyssa's driveway, and her hair went limp. Hailey and Alyssa ran up to greet her and ask how she'd been.

"I just moved onto Draco Drive a few days ago," Madison referred to a road off Orion Street.

"So how do you like the middle school?" asked Alyssa.

"Oh, I go to Catholic school now," said Madison. "What about you?"

"Hailey and I are homeschooled now," said Alyssa. "I never got to tell you."

"That's okay," said Madison. "So you guys want to come over to my house on Saturday?"

"What time?" asked Alyssa.

"I'll ask my mom and let you know," said Madison. "Okay, bye, guys. Nice seeing you again." She rode back in the direction she'd come from as Hailey and Alyssa waved goodbye to her.

After washing the car for another ten minutes, Alyssa and Hailey cleaned up and walked back inside. A snore suggested to Alyssa that Mrs. Hutchinson slept. Huh? She never napped while babysitting.

Alyssa strode toward the living room and saw Mrs. Hutchinson asleep on one of the couches. Hailey followed her. "Why is Mrs. Hutchinson sleeping?"

"I don't know," said Alyssa.

"Can you show me the note?"

Alyssa nodded and led her up the stairs. She opened her door but gasped at what she saw. The note that she'd left on her bed was gone.

"Where's the note?" asked Hailey.

"It was right there," Alyssa pointed to the bed.

But another piece of paper appeared onto the mattress. Alyssa picked it up and read it.

Hello again, Alyssa,

I have put your babysitter to sleep to reveal magic to you. You'll find out why she is sleeping later.

Anonymous

"Not again," mumbled Alyssa. "Why won't they say their name?" She showed the note to Hailey.

"Let's go call my dad before anything happens," said Hailey.

How much worse could this get? Alyssa thought as she followed Hailey down the stairs.

2

Entering the first floor, the girls continued toward the phone. But they stopped and turned to Mrs. Hutchinson. Parts of her hair turned green now. Black rings circled her eyes. Not only that—a piece of paper also appeared onto the wall outside the living room. Alyssa and Hailey approached it and gasped at the messages, which looked like they'd been typed.

I sprayed my babysitter's hair with spray paint — Alyssa McCarthy

I drew dark circles around my babysitter's eyes with a black magic marker — Hailey Flynn

"We better take this off." Hailey pulled on a corner and grunted. It stayed stuck as if attached with permanent glue.

"It's not coming off!" she squeaked.

"We're going to have to call your dad."

"Do you still have the note?"

"Yeah." Alyssa reached into her pants pocket. But she felt nothing. "What the heck? It, like, disappeared!"

"What? Are you kidding me?"

"Let's call your dad." Alyssa turned to the phone. But a door slamming shut suggested to her that Uncle Bruce had come home. She and Hailey turned around as he carried his bags.

"What are you two doing near the phone?" he asked since every phone call had to be earned except during emergencies.

"We need to tell you something!" shrieked Hailey.

"Why are you screaming, Hailey?" asked Uncle Bruce.

"Because—"

"Oh my god, girls, what did you do?" screeched Mrs. Hutchinson.

Everyone turned to her.

"We didn't do it!" yelled Hailey.

"Then why does this piece of paper say you did?" Mrs. Hutchinson pointed at it.

Uncle Bruce power-walked toward it and heaved a gasp. "Oh my goodness!" He glared at the girls. "Alyssa Caitlin McCarthy and Hailey Elizabeth Flynn, what were you thinking?"

"Hailey's right!" cried Alyssa. "We didn't do it!"

"Don't you dare lie to me!" snarled Uncle Bruce. "No one was here besides you!" He pulled a corner and struggled to remove it. "What did you do?"

"We didn't do anything!" screamed Hailey.

"Stop lying!" boomed Uncle Bruce. "What's the matter with you two? Why would you make marks on Mrs. Hutchinson? Are you three years old? No! You both are way too old to do what you've just done!" He turned to Mrs. Hutchinson. "Lorraine, you cannot sleep while babysitting!"

"I . . . I—"

"You're fired!" Uncle Bruce said. "Get your stuff and go!"

Mrs. Hutchinson inhaled and exhaled and walked toward the closet.

Uncle Bruce leaned down and grasped Alyssa's narrow shoulders. She clenched her teeth since Uncle Bruce's grip hurt. His brittle salt-and-pepper hair even touched and scratched her forehead. She squinted her eyes.

"You are going to be thirteen next month!" Uncle Bruce bellowed. "Yet you and Hailey did something so childish and then lied to me!"

"We really didn't do it!" cried Alyssa. "I'm not lying!"

"Then how else would those marks have gotten there?" asked Uncle Bruce.

"M-magic," answered Alyssa.

Uncle Bruce slapped her cheek.

"Ow!" Alyssa rubbed that section.

"That is the dumbest answer I've heard!" Uncle Bruce turned to Hailey, squeezing her narrow shoulders like he had done to Alyssa. "Hailey, don't you lie to me, either!"

"Dad, please listen to us!"

"Absolutely not!" He let go. "I am now going to lock the study door so that neither of you can get inside without my permission!"

"Uncle Bruce, I swear we—"

"Shut up, Alyssa!" he rumbled. "You and Hailey are now grounded for two months!"

"No!" squeaked Alyssa.

"I'm sorry that you won't be enjoying your birthday, Alyssa, but you should've thought of that before spray-painting Mrs. Hutchinson's hair and lying to me."

"How many times do I have to tell you that we didn't do it?" Hailey stomped.

"I don't want to hear it anymore!" thundered Uncle Bruce. "I'm also giving you more work for homeschooling tomorrow!"

"Dad—"

"Go to your rooms and stay there until dinner!" Uncle Bruce pointed to the stairs.

Alyssa and Hailey dragged their feet up the steps. They burst into tears, reaching the top. Alyssa's worry had come true. All she wanted to do was prove Uncle Bruce wrong. Would the evidence of magic ever appear?

Alyssa entered her room and threw herself onto her bed. She sobbed and curled up into a ball. Tears even streamed down to her quilt. That mysterious *person* deserved the blame. He or she should lose privileges forever. Alyssa wished to escape this house. She wanted her godfather to let her live with him as soon as possible.

Even though her godfather could've been her legal guardian, Alyssa had moved here because Emily, her babysitter at the time her parents had died, had babysat Hailey too. Emily had convinced the police to let her take Alyssa to her aunt and uncle's house to stay for the night. Emily had also obtained Aunt Laura and Uncle Bruce's consent over her cell phone. After Alyssa had settled here with them, they had become her legal guardians.

Because her godfather hadn't been able to attend her baptism when she was a baby, her church had baptized her again when she was five. From then on, she and her godfather had shared a strong bond. He had sent her gifts during holidays and special occasions and had taken her on fun trips.

He'd moved from Ohio to New Jersey after becoming her godparent so that he could've been near her church. But shortly after she had moved in with her aunt and uncle, he'd found a job in Ohio and had moved back. However, he had still called and e-mailed Alyssa every now and then.

All she wanted to do was talk to him. But she couldn't right now. Her mind switched to Aunt Laura. She wished she and Hailey had never bought that chocolate box for Valentine's Day three years ago.

When Alyssa and Hailey were in the fourth and third grade, Aunt Laura had run Hailey's class as the class mom. Because Hailey's classmates had appreciated her sympathy, they'd all given her candy gifts for Valentine's Day.

The box Alyssa and Hailey had bought had contained no flavor charts on the outside. So when Aunt Laura had opened the box and looked at the labels, she had aimed for a milk-chocolate truffle filled with caramel. But she had accidentally touched a dark-chocolate truffle filled with raspberry. She'd had a fatal allergy to berries. Her face had reddened, her throat had constricted, which had decreased her ability to breathe, and then she had collapsed. Before the ambulance had arrived at the house, though, Aunt Laura had died.

Uncle Bruce's depression had led him to blame Hailey and Alyssa for her death since they'd never warned her not to touch the chocolate that had looked like it'd been filled with raspberry. His stress had increased enough that he could never move on and treat them the way he'd used to. He'd placed new rules on Alyssa and Hailey that they'd disagreed with and still loathed now.

He'd even lost trust in so many other people whom he thought "spoiled" them with free fun since he believed it had to be earned. In fact, he'd pulled Alyssa and Hailey out of school last June because he'd thought that recess, friends, and other enjoyable times had distracted them from achieving acceptable results on their assignments. Starting last spring, the two hadn't gotten past Bs, and Uncle Bruce expected straight As. That'd been when he'd decided that all those "distractions" had ruined them. When Alyssa was in fifth grade, he had pulled her out of tap, jazz, and ballet classes because her teacher had rewarded all the ballet students with lollipops. Despite her and Hailey's thin bodies, Uncle Bruce only allowed earned junk food a few times a year, and it couldn't be sweet or exceed a few hundred calories.

Uncle Bruce didn't scare Alyssa and Hailey as if he were a monster. In fact, he allowed them to buy stylish clothes, even if they cost a lot. But he wouldn't let them have any electronic devices. He believed that they would be too expensive and that the girls would become addicted to them. He let them use the computer in the study but only to write and print their assigned papers. They couldn't use the Internet except to look up information related to their schoolwork. He'd also disconnected the TV since he'd found it distracting, and he had claimed that it had affected the girls' ability to learn.

Alyssa pulled out her old photo album from the bookshelf and brought it to her bed. She turned the page to a picture of herself at the age of eight, Hailey at the age of seven, and Aunt Laura. They all stood with her in front of a place called Piper's Village, which contained old-fashioned shops.

Aunt Laura's diamond-white smile glistened like a midnight star. Freckles spotted her face. Chestnut curls spiraled to her shoulders. Wispy bangs hid her forehead. Everything about her made Alyssa miss her, including her cooking. Aunt Laura used to bake delicious double-chocolate-chip cookies, lasagna, and chicken parmesan. Uncle Bruce, however, only cooked plain white meat, fish, and vegetables and sometimes prepared salads. He'd never grilled burgers, boiled pasta, or baked desserts after Aunt Laura had died.

"Dinner's ready!" Uncle Bruce called to Alyssa and Hailey. The two went downstairs. Uncle Bruce had prepared grilled chicken over Swiss chard, arugula, leaf lettuce, avocado, onions, and chopped tomatoes. He forbade dressing unless they were vinegar based. But he'd run out two days ago.

"Okay, girls, time to eat," he said. "I want your plates cleaned before you go to bed."

Alyssa sighed, sitting down. She couldn't bring up that incident again unless more magic came.

She ate her salad, and the phone rang.

Uncle Bruce hurried over to answer. "Hello?"

Alyssa continued to consume her food and ignore him. He probably talked to someone she didn't know.

"Hey, Mr. Steinberg, how are you?"

Alyssa still tuned out.

"Great. So you'll tutor Alyssa and Hailey from three-thirty to five tomorrow?"

All right. Mr. Steinberg was a tutor, so Alyssa paid attention to Uncle Bruce.

"Okay, text me the directions to your house. I'll see you tomorrow. Bye." He hung up.

"Dad, is that guy going to tutor us?" asked Hailey.

"By 'that guy,' you mean Mr. Steinberg," Uncle Bruce said. "And yes, he will be tutoring you tomorrow. In fact, every Friday from three-thirty to five."

"Why?" asked Hailey.

"Because even in homeschooling, your grades still aren't that good. All you get are Bs and Cs. I want straight As."

"What's wrong with Bs?" asked Hailey.

"They're below my standards. We're not the only family like that, though. Lots of other parents expect straight A's."

"I really don't think Bs are that bad," said Alyssa.

"Well, I do," said Uncle Bruce. "Now finish your dinner. No more talking until everything on your plate is gone."

Alyssa sighed, piercing a piece of grilled chicken with her fork. Uncle Bruce had relaxed his attitude more, but that meant nothing. Alyssa still wouldn't get to visit Madison on Saturday. She would get to have nothing her way, and tomorrow, she'd receive a heavy load of work from Uncle Bruce.

3

Last night Alyssa had set her alarm for seven o'clock in the morning so that she could talk to Alex. Uncle Bruce had sent her and Hailey to bed right after dinner. Every time she'd tried to enter kitchen, Uncle Bruce still worked in there. At one point, Alyssa had struggled to stay awake and had fallen asleep.

Her alarm rang, so she shut it off. She hopped out of bed, sweating in her flannel pajama pants and long-sleeved purple shirt. She'd change after talking to Alex.

Cracking the door open, Alyssa peeked out and looked around. Silence filled the hallway. Alyssa stepped outside and crept toward the staircase. Despite the quiet, tingles still prickled her skin. She hoped to avoid getting caught aiming for the kitchen phone.

She stepped on the top step and walked down. She quickened breaths out of her mouth as she approached the middle of the staircase. But she made her way to the first floor without disturbing Uncle Bruce or Hailey.

She looked back, checking to see if either one had woken up. There were no sounds or movements. Okay—good. She headed into the kitchen to look up Alex's number.

Alyssa picked up the phonebook from a drawer and flipped the pages to the K tab. She found names like Keenan, Khan, and Kriesberg but no sign of the name, Alexander Kress.

How could his contact information be unavailable? Alyssa would check her e-mail—except that Uncle Bruce had locked the study last night. She sighed, putting the phonebook back. Did anything else contain Alex's phone number? Even though she had never been able to find it or even convince Uncle Bruce to let her talk to him, she resumed searching.

Sorting through the stationery, Alyssa saw old letters from earlier this year, vendor brochures, and some envelopes. No luck—until she thought she saw a double S on the last envelope. Pulling it out, she saw the name, Alex Kress, on it.

She looked inside and saw a folded piece of paper. She opened it and saw that it'd been written a week after her parents had died.

January 22, 2005

Dear Laura,

My heart still breaks for you after hearing about the deaths of Ashton and Clara. I can imagine how much it hurt to lose your younger brother and his wife at the hands of a drunk driver. And poor Alyssa—seven is just far too young to be left without parents.

I'm glad Emily was able to convince the cops to let her take Alyssa to your house. I wish all nineteen-year-old babysitters had that power in them.

Please accept my sincere sympathy and take good care of Alyssa. If something happens again, let me know since I am her godfather.

Wishing you peace and healing,

Alex Kress

P.S. If you need to reach me, my house address is 50 Gemini Road, Brock Hills, Ohio, and my phone number is 740-555-7722.

Alyssa formed a weak smile. She picked up the phone and dialed his number. Then she walked into the living room with the phone up to her ear.

"Hello?" Alex answered.

"Hey, Alex, it's Alyssa, your goddaughter."

"Alyssa? Really?"

"Yes. I . . . I . . ."

"I haven't heard from you in three years. What's been going on?"

"It . . . It's my uncle."

"What about him?"

Alyssa spent several minutes explaining how Uncle Bruce had changed and how he'd treated her and Hailey since Aunt Laura's death.

"Oh my god, I can't believe that," said Alex.

"My uncle even grounded us for something we didn't do."

"What was it?"

"Um . . . it may sound stupid to you."

"Still—it would help me if you said it anyway."

"All right." Alyssa breathed and told him the reason.

"Magic?"

"Yes, Alex. Hailey saw it too. If she were standing here right now, I'd have her tell you."

There was another halt. Alex breathed.

"I'm sorry, b-but it's the truth."

"Oh... m-my god," gasped Alex. "I . . . I don't believe it."

"Yeah, I didn't believe in it, either. But can you keep magic a secret from anyone else you know?"

"I don't think anyone will believe me anyway. But sure, sweetie. I won't tell anybody."

"Thanks. No one other than Hailey believed me. So anyway, when can you talk to your lawyer about having me move in with you?"

"I can do it now, but it'll take at least a month before I can be your guardian."

"What?"

"Yeah. I'm sorry. If I could make it earlier, I would. But that's what I've read."

Alyssa sighed. "Okay."

"I'll work out what I can, all right?"

"Sure. I love you." Alyssa hung up.

"Alyssa?" Hailey called from upstairs.

"Yeah?"

"Who were you talking to?" Hailey walked down the steps.

"If I tell you, do you promise not to tell your dad?"

"Yes."

"My godfather."

Hailey raised her eyebrows and opened her mouth. "You actually got to talk to him?"

Alyssa nodded.

"If you get to live with him, will I be able to go too?"

"Sorry, no."

"Why not?"

"The way my parents had organized it was for him to be only my guardian."

Hailey groaned.

"It's okay, Hailey, you can talk to your grandparents. They only live a half hour away."

"Yeah, I guess I could."

"Girls, get dressed!" Uncle Bruce shouted from upstairs.

"I'll call them later," Hailey said.

The two headed back up. Alyssa walked into her room, where she dressed herself in jeggings, a tank top, and a plaid shirt. She heard another swish and turned to her bed. It had better not have come from the anonymous sender again. Nevertheless, Alyssa picked up the paper and read it.

Dear Alyssa,

We need to talk about the strange happenings you encountered yesterday. I didn't commit them, but I know who did. The name of the person is Beau Duchamp. I will tell you all about it in a few minutes. Meet me in your bathroom. The one you're closest to.

See you soon,
Simon

P.S. If you're wondering why Duchamp and I made these notes appear to you, it's because that's how we wizards communicate with people when we don't know their contact information.

Alyssa breathed. She could now show the name of the person who'd committed those crazy pranks to Uncle Bruce. But who was this Simon guy? How did he know her name? He sounded like a trustworthy person. But when Alyssa had learned about stranger safety as a little kid, adults had taught her never to trust strangers. Still, maybe she should give listening to Simon a try. Whenever somebody showed care and offered guidance, Alyssa had always trusted him or her. But she'd already known those people.

She walked into the bathroom to do her morning routine: wash her face and brush her hair and teeth. But a voice with an English accent whispered, "Alyssa, don't go."

Alyssa turned around, letting out a shriek. A small marble statue with wings, short wavy hair, and a suit stood by her. He waved.

"I know—I look strange," said the statue.

"You're . . . you're—"

"Simon—the one who sent you the note about this meeting," he said.

"You should've told me you're a statue." Alyssa knelt down.

Simon bent his eyebrows. "Who are you calling a statue? Statues aren't alive. Therefore, I'm *not* a statue."

"Then what are you?" asked Alyssa.

"A marble figure," Simon answered. "I've been alive for thirty years. In fact, I was born into a family of marble figures."

"How did marble figures come to life?"

"Some wizard magically brought them to life two thousand years ago. I don't know how, but I don't have time to tell you anyway. We need to discuss Duchamp and the storm tonight."

"There's going to be a storm?"

"Yes." Simon turned to the door. "Hey, why don't you lock the door? I can't be seen."

Alyssa did so. "So why didn't anyone tell me about the storm?"

"Duchamp is forming it now."

"Was he the one who turned the rain black and—"

"Yes. He committed every magical incident from yesterday."

"Including the marks on my babysitter?"

"Yep. He's also responsible for making her fall asleep."

"My uncle grounded my cousin and me for that." Alyssa lowered her voice.

"I'm sorry to hear." Simon frowned. "I'm assuming you also told him the truth and he didn't believe you."

Alyssa nodded.

"Well, just like Duchamp wanted your babysitter gone, he wants to hurt your uncle now too."

Alyssa gasped.

"That's why he's creating the storm. It was the best thing he could think of. Right now, he's hiding somewhere. He doesn't want anyone to see him until you have no one to protect you."

"Can't the police find him?"

"Nope. He's so powerful that he created charms on himself to make him invisible to the police and government—from anywhere in the world."

"What the heck?"

"I know. Anyway, let's talk about the storm. Tonight it's supposed to sleet in bright colors."

Alyssa brightened her eyes. "Why?"

"So people will get worried. But it's going to hurt your uncle in some way. I don't know how, though."

"Something's going to happen to him tonight?"

"Yes."

"Oh my god," moaned Alyssa. Despite how Uncle Bruce had been, Alyssa still realized that she loved him and would never want anything to hurt to him.

"But most importantly, Alyssa, you need to know about what Duchamp wants with you."

"What?"

"He wants to kidnap you and bring you to the Fiji Islands to enslave you."

Alyssa inhaled, tightening her chest. "You're kidding."

"I wish. But he owns a dark magic center there, and he wants to keep you there. Magical connections work better in the tropics, and Duchamp can only achieve his goal if he weakens you there with some type of magic."

"Wait—there's a connection between us?"

"Yes. He received it last fall at your parents' graves when he put a magic thermos near it and sucked in copies of their DNA."

Alyssa lowered her jaw. "Why did he do that?"

"I don't know. I'll have to find out. But once he opened the lid, the DNA evaporated and traveled to you since you're the only one related to them that he could use."

Alyssa kept her jaw hanging and tilted herself back. "I don't remember that."

"It happened when you were sleeping. It doesn't work when you're awake. But since then, the magic in the connection has grown and reached its peak yesterday."

Alyssa clenched her teeth. "Oh no." She inhaled and exhaled.

"Yes, I know how it feels. But one of the good things about marble figures is that we can absorb information from other people's brains. So later today I'll talk to you about why he wants you exactly."

"Wait, you can what?"

"Don't worry, Alyssa. I only gather information to help people. I don't absorb anything else."

"You sure?"

"Of course."

"Okay."

"I'm going to go now." Simon pushed his body up into the air.

"Wait, when will I see you again?"

"Soon." He held out his arms and disappeared.

Alyssa breathed and her heartbeat rushed. She left the bathroom and headed downstairs for breakfast. Uncle Bruce cooked spinach and egg-white omelets, and Hailey ate some sliced pears.

"What were you doing upstairs for so long?" asked Hailey.

"Uh . . . hanging out," Alyssa said. "Did anyone hear about the storm tonight?"

"What storm?" asked Hailey.

"It's supposed to sleet," said Alyssa.

"They didn't say anything about sleet on the radio," said Uncle Bruce. "I don't know where you heard that, but you need to let that go and eat your breakfast. We've got a lot of work to cover today."

Alyssa sat at the table and had the pears. At some point, the radio should announce the storm. Uncle Bruce must also learn that it would harm him tonight. Alyssa would rather let him know as soon as possible than at the last minute.

.

4

A knock on the door made Alyssa jump back in her desk chair. Only twenty minutes had passed since today's homeschooling had ended. Alyssa hadn't even finished a quarter of her homework load. According to her digital clock, it was three.

Uncle Bruce opened the door and poked his head inside. "Get ready, Alyssa. We need to be at Mr. Steinberg's in a half hour."

"What should I bring?" she asked.

"Nothing. He's going to give you work."

"Are you kidding me?" Alyssa followed Uncle Bruce downstairs.

"Don't worry. You'll be finished with it before you come home. He's not giving you homework."

"Okay, good." Alyssa joined Hailey and walked with her and Uncle Bruce out the door.

Despite the storm that would happen tonight, the weather didn't cool her at all. In fact, it had warmed up to around the high fifties or low sixties.

Alyssa hopped into the back seat with Hailey, and Uncle Bruce slid into the driver's seat.

"Can you put the radio on?" asked Alyssa.

"Why?" asked Uncle Bruce.

"Because of the storm tonight."

Uncle Bruce sighed and started the car. He turned on the radio and selected the news station, where the meteorologist discussed the weather forecast. It would lower into the twenties tonight.

Okay, that's a good sign of letting people know about the storm, Alyssa thought.

The weatherman announced that it would sleet up to three inches. He also said that there might be power outages as early as seven or eight o'clock tonight. But he mentioned nothing about the sleet's vivid colors. The weather forecast concluded.

"You were right, Alyssa," said Uncle Bruce. "There is going to be a storm."

"Yeah, the sleet's even going to be funny colors," Alyssa said. "The weatherman just forgot to say that."

"Alyssa, don't talk like that," Uncle Bruce said. "Sleet can't be any color but white."

"How do you even know that?" asked Hailey.

"I heard it somewhere," said Alyssa.

"Where?" asked Uncle Bruce.

"From . . . someone," said Alyssa.

"Who?" Uncle Bruce asked.

"A . . . uh . . . talking marble figure."

"Alyssa, stop it right now!" exclaimed Uncle Bruce. "How many times do I have to remind you there is no such thing as magic?"

"Yes, there is," Alyssa said.

"I'm not arguing with you. So let's stop talking about this right now."

Alyssa heaved a sigh. Would she ever get a chance to tell him that he'd be harmed?

"Now, girls, I want you on your best behavior at Mr. Steinberg's. He's not like many other tutors."

"What do you mean?" asked Hailey.

"He's much stricter."

"Are you kidding me?" asked Alyssa. "Uncle Bruce, I've had enough of—"

"Alyssa, don't you understand that strictness is actually a good thing? A strict tutor will only help you get better."

"So you're saying that if I had an easygoing tutor, I wouldn't get better?"

"I'm not saying that, but it'd be unlikely for you to improve as much as if you had a strict tutor."

Alyssa sighed again. She'd had enough of that attitude. In school, she had had some easygoing teachers, but ever since she'd left, she had experienced nobody laid back watching her.

Minutes had gone by. Uncle Bruce turned onto Libra Court and parked at the fourth house in. Everybody hopped out and walked to the front door. Uncle Bruce rang the doorbell, and a frowning man wearing round glasses answered. A bushy gray mustache drooped passed his mouth, making his frown appear larger. Alyssa inhaled and exhaled. This guy would probably behave more like Uncle Bruce and Mrs. Hutchinson.

"Hello, I'm Augustus Steinberg."

"Bruce Flynn." Uncle Bruce shook hands with Mr. Steinberg.

Alyssa and Hailey followed Mr. Steinberg inside. He sat them in his living room.

"So I'll be done with them at five o'clock, okay?" Mr. Steinberg said.

"I'll be here by then." Uncle Bruce returned to the car.

Mr. Steinberg closed the door. "I need to make a phone call before we get started. Also, we have another girl joining us today."

"Who's that?" asked Hailey.

"Her name's Destiny Cox," answered Mr. Steinberg. "I was able to squeeze her in."

Destiny Cox? That girl from Alyssa's old elementary school that used to pick on her? Now that Alyssa had been pulled out of the school, Destiny had new reasons to bully her. Mr. Steinberg could catch Destiny and discipline her, however. Then Alyssa would support his rules and attitude—unless Destiny succeeded at hiding her taunting or teasing.

The doorbell rang, and Mr. Steinberg answered it. Destiny and her mother stood outside. Mr. Steinberg greeted them.

"Mom, do I have to go?"

"Destiny Leigh Cox, do you want me to ground you for another week?" her mom asked.

"No."

"So please cooperate," said Mrs. Cox.

She left, and Destiny stepped inside. Alyssa clapped her hand under her chin and arched her eyebrows. Mrs. Cox had punished Destiny for a *week*—yet Destiny had more behavioral problems.

Mr. Steinberg pointed at the living room and repeated to Destiny what he'd told Alyssa and Hailey. Destiny walked toward Alyssa and Hailey. She smiled and flicked her long dark-brown braids behind her shoulders.

"Hello, losers." She sat down. "How's life now without any friends?"

"We still have friends," Hailey said.

"Yeah, Madison said hi to me yesterday," said Alyssa.

"Well, Madison doesn't go to Bursnell anymore," said Destiny.

"So?" asked Alyssa.

"Do any of your other friends say hi or call you *besides* Madison?"

Alyssa exhaled.

"Ha! I knew it! They don't care about you anymore. In fact, they all have boyfriends now."

"Shut up, Destiny," said Alyssa.

"No! You shut up, nerd!"

"Leave her alone," said Hailey.

"Yeah, Destiny, please stop," said Alyssa.

"You're not the boss of me."

"Still," said Alyssa.

"What do you mean, 'still'?" asked Destiny. "You're not a teenager yet. You're still a preteen. *I've* been a teenager for three months. So I'm older than you."

"Not by such a big difference," said Hailey. "Alyssa is turning thirteen next month."

"Girls, it's time!" Mr. Steinberg called from the staircase.

The girls stood up and followed Mr. Steinberg up the stairs to a small room. Dirt and dust covered the gray carpet. The walls were painted lemon yellow, as if Mr. Steinberg didn't want his students to relax. Despite the filthy carpet and bright-colored wall, Mr. Steinberg's desk had nothing on it except piles of paper and a desktop computer.

Mr. Steinberg started the session by going over the rules. Alyssa didn't mind the rules of no eating or drinking, no using electronics, and only one bathroom break per person each hour. However, if she were to get distracted, Mr. Steinberg would smack a ruler on the desk side in front of her.

"All right, girls, I'm going to give you some reading booklets," said Mr. Steinberg. "According to your parents, you all need help with English comprehension." He distributed one to each girl. "The first two times, I'm going to read the stories. But after that, you're on your own."

About the expected amount of time had passed. Alyssa finished working on the last math problem in her booklet.

Mr. Steinberg said, "All right, girls, pencils down."

They all stopped working.

"The session has ended," said Mr. Steinberg. "You may go downstairs and wait for your parents."

The girls stood up and headed out of the room. When Alyssa approached the staircase, she heard another swish. Looking down, she saw a small sticky note at her feet. She picked it up and read it.

Hi Alyssa,

You may meet me in the bathroom on the second floor now.

Cheers,
Simon

"Alyssa, what are you doing?" asked Mr. Steinberg.

"Um . . ." Alyssa shoved the note into her jeggings pocket. "Can I go to the bathroom?"

"Yes. Go down till you reach the last door on your right."

Alyssa walked toward the bathroom. Stepping inside, she turned the lights on—but gasped at Simon, who stood still. He inhaled and jumped back.   "Blimey, Alyssa, you scared me."

"Sorry," she said. "So did you get all the information about why Duchamp wants me?"

"Yep. I also tried to get some information about what Duchamp wants to do with your uncle. But he's still thinking about it."

"Oh boy."

"I wish I could stop him." Simon paused. "Now let me talk about why Duchamp wants you. It all started back in the spring of 1982, when Duchamp and his wife, who's dead now, had a baby named Jacque, who was a maglack."

"What's a maglack?"

"A person born into a wizarding family with no magical skills or abilities. Anyway, Duchamp and his wife were worried about him growing up with wizards and how he would have a tough time. So they put him up for adoption. He was adopted a year and a half later by an American family, and his new name became Derrick Wesley."

Alyssa gasped. "T-that was the name of the guy who killed my parents."

"I'll get to that later. When his son was adopted, Duchamp used a special magical device that could receive the images and personal information of his son's new adoptive parents. But it wouldn't be able to track his actions until he found that he was adopted."

"When was that?"

"Early October 2004, a month after he moved into your neighborhood. I was able to absorb that too. Anyhow, Derrick was so angry that he became a troublemaker."

"How'd he find out that he was adopted?"

"He was at a family reunion, and his adopted father drank a little too much." Simon exhaled "He let that secret slip. Anyway, do you remember receiving opened packages of candy drizzled with soap when you were seven?"

"Yeah. It was in a gift pouch outside the Wesleys' house."

"That was from Derrick."

"My mom yelled at him on the phone the next day, and I couldn't get everything she said."

"All the neighbors yelled at him. From then on… he got terrible drinking problems. The night he killed your parents—he drank too much."

"I'm never going to forget that." Alyssa covered her head.

"No one does." Simon shook his head. "But Duchamp had found out everything on the Internet when he searched for Derrick Wesley on Google. He was so upset and did something so horrible and illegal… the French wizarding government exiled him to Australia."

"Why did he move to the Fiji Islands then?"

"He moved there a few months after. In Australia's wizarding communities, the government was strong enough to track every harmful spell and arrest any wizard who cast one. He couldn't hide from them."

"Good."

That was why he moved to the Fiji Islands, where he could cast charms to block the government and police from finding him."

"But he waited until last fall to go to my parents' graves?"

"He was too busy working on his dark magic center."

"What the—"

"Yep, he was also hiring people to work for him, and he built a magical computer. He tested the charms too. But they were so hard to create, so he didn't make them fully until last September."

Alyssa sighed and her eyes watered. "Why did he go to my parents' graves?"

"He had become so stressed that he had trouble being logical with his reasons. He decided to blame your parents for Derrick's arrest."

Alyssa covered her mouth.

"Duchamp also decided to blame them for his major stress and depression. He's just had so many issues."

"That's terrible." Alyssa smeared her eyes.

"He decided that he needed to harm you so that he could go back to France and became a major tyrant to take revenge on the French government. When a wizard or maglack kills someone, either magically or not, the family members on both sides are eligible to form connections. And only if the last family member is weakened can the sorcerer become extremely powerful. If Duchamp doesn't weaken you, he'll never be able to overpower the French government."

"But then why does he want to take me to the Fiji Islands?"

"Besides the reason I told you last time we met, the killing spell doesn't work anymore. It was blocked six years ago when a massive wizarding war took place in Russia. The international magic control let out charms to the magic satellite in space to block it from being used."

"So if he's invisible to the police and government, then how can I report him?"

"I don't know. You might not be able to."

There was a knock on the door. Alyssa gasped. "Yeah?"

"Your uncle's here," said Mr. Steinberg.

"Coming," said Alyssa.

"I'll send you another note about the incidents so that you can show your uncle," whispered Simon. He pushed himself into the air. He held out his arms and disappeared.

Alyssa rushed out the bathroom and down the stairs. Hailey and Uncle Bruce stood by the door.

"Let's go," said Uncle Bruce.

Alyssa followed him and Hailey to the car.

5

"Are you okay, Alyssa?" Hailey asked as Uncle Bruce backed out of Mr. Steinberg's driveway.

"I . . . um . . . have some stuff to say," said Alyssa.

"What?" asked Hailey.

"I saw the talking marble figure again and—"

"Alyssa McCarthy, stop making things up," said Uncle Bruce.

"I'm not making it up," she said. "I really did see a talking marble figure. He told me—"

"Since when did you start making imaginary friends again?" asked Uncle Bruce.

"He's not imaginary," said Alyssa.

"All right, that's enough." Uncle Bruce put the radio on, and the news played.

Alyssa crossed her arms. Uncle Bruce had to know that someone hunted both him and her down and that the storm would do something horrible to *him*. Simon should send her the note about the incidents as soon as possible. But why couldn't he do it now?

The news story concluded, and the weather forecast began. Alyssa listened to everything the weatherman could say about the storm, but he only repeated what he'd said last time. Nothing about the sleet's colors mentioned. Darn. Now until Simon sent the note, Alyssa would have no proof to show that magic existed.

Uncle Bruce's cell phone rang, and he answered it with his Bluetooth earpiece. "Hello?"

Alyssa tuned out, assuming he spoke to someone she didn't know or that he would say nothing to her.

"There's a meeting at the office today?" asked Uncle Bruce.

Okay, this caught Alyssa's attention. Uncle Bruce worked on Tuesdays, Thursdays, and alternate Saturdays in a lawyer's office from three to five as well as an online job during the whole week. He homeschooled the girls for the rest of the time except on Sundays and his off-Saturdays. Now that a meeting would occur, he'd either have to say that he couldn't go or have to find someone to look after Alyssa and Hailey.

"But what about the storm?" asked Uncle Bruce.

Right. Why would a meeting be scheduled when a strange storm was coming?

"It'll only be a half hour? Can't you move it?"

Alyssa kept watching and listening, wondering what the answer would be.

"Okay. I'll be there at six. Bye." He hung up. "Girls, I have to go to a meeting at work. But since you no longer have a babysitter and I obviously can't leave you home alone, I have to text a bunch of people to see who's available to look after you now."

"But, Dad, you can't text and drive," Hailey said.

"No, but I *can* pull over and text," Uncle Bruce said. Uncle Bruce did so. After about a minute, his phone made its texting sound, and he answered it.

"Okay, girls, only one person is available now," he said. "It's my friend, Mrs. Wilson." He pulled back onto the street.

After a short while, Uncle Bruce turned onto Scorpio Lane. Alyssa's nerves twisted. She wondered what Mrs. Wilson would be like. If Mrs. Hutchinson and Mr. Steinberg both had attitudes she disliked, then Mrs. Wilson might too.

Uncle Bruce parked at the third to last house on the left. Alyssa and Hailey followed him to the door. He rang the doorbell.

A light-brown-skinned woman with puffy shoulder-length hair opened the door, smiling at Bruce. This couldn't be Mrs. Wilson, even if anybody could have an English name. But—just because she grinned at Uncle Bruce, that didn't necessarily mean she'd show sympathy to Alyssa and Hailey.

"Hi, Bruce." She pulled Uncle Bruce into a hug.

"Hello, Janine." Uncle Bruce let go of her and turned to Hailey and Alyssa. "Girls, this is Mrs. Wilson."

Alyssa and Hailey introduced themselves.

"I'll be back in about an hour, Janine," said Uncle Bruce.

"Okay, Bruce," said Mrs. Wilson. "Bye."

Mrs. Wilson took the girls' coats and shoes and placed them in her closet. She led them into the kitchen. The smell of steak cooking in the oven filled the air.

"That smells good," said Alyssa.

"You and Hailey are welcome to have some," said Mrs. Wilson.

"Cool," Alyssa said.

"We are supposed to lose power anyway," said Mrs. Wilson. "So you might as well eat dinner here."

"Thanks." Alyssa smiled.

"The steak won't be ready for another twenty to twenty-five minutes, though," said Mrs. Wilson. "But in the meantime, I can give you something else to eat."

"What do you have?" Hailey asked.

Mrs. Wilson opened her refrigerator. "I have leftover macaroni and cheese, fruit, yogurt—"

"I'll have the mac and cheese, please." Alyssa jumped.

"Okay. Hailey, what do you want?"

"Uh . . . not fruit or—"

"You want me to make you a sandwich?" asked Mrs. Wilson. "I can make you grilled cheese, tuna, bologna, peanut butter and jelly—"

"Alyssa's allergic to peanuts," said Hailey. "I don't want her to get an allergic reaction."

"Hailey, I'm only a *little* bit allergic," Alyssa said.

"Still, I don't want you near anything you're allergic to," said Mrs. Wilson.

In kindergarten, Alyssa's class had held a peanut-butter-and-jelly-sandwich-making day. Kids and parents had brought in different kinds of the three main ingredients. Because Alyssa's dad had had a deathly peanut allergy, she hadn't brought in anything. She'd still tried a sandwich, though. But bumps had formed around her upper lip and chin. Her throat had also narrowed. The teacher had rushed her to the nurse and had called her mom. After Alyssa's mother had given her medicine, Alyssa had recovered. Her mom had realized the peanuts had caused her reaction because she'd eaten toast and jam before with no problem. An allergy test right after had also confirmed the peanut issue. Since then, Alyssa had never touched peanuts again.

While the macaroni and cheese warmed up, Mrs. Wilson made Hailey's tuna sandwich. She also served Alyssa some orange juice and Hailey some seltzer. They ate everything given to them.

Mrs. Wilson arched her eyebrows at the opening that led to the kitchen. A little boy no older than seven or eight waved a Blackberry phone in the air. "I've got your phone, I've got your phone," he chanted.

"Stop it!" snapped a teenage girl's voice. The girl grabbed it out of the boy's hand.

Mrs. Wilson strode toward them. "Leon Roger Wilson and Jasmine Nicole Wilson, knock it off!" She glared at Jasmine.

"Jasmine, you're turning fifteen in August! You're too old to grab from your little brother's hand!" She turned to Leon. "Leon, you're eight years old now, so it's time you start showing some big-boy behavior!"

Leon groaned. "Fine."

"Now why don't you two say hi to my friend, Mr. Flynn's, daughter and niece?" asked Mrs. Wilson.

Jasmine and Leon introduced themselves to Alyssa and Hailey.

A swish came from the ground. Alyssa found a note and picked it up, but she stayed ducked under the table.

Dear Alyssa,

Please tell your uncle that the storm will harm him tonight and what I told you about Duchamp if you haven't done so already. I will send him a note about the incidents in a few minutes.

Don't worry. He'll believe you once he sees the note appear.

Cheers,
Simon

Alyssa put the note into her jeggings pocket and sat up again.

"What were you doing, Alyssa?" asked Hailey.

Alyssa leaned into her ear and whispered the answer.

Hailey gasped. "Why didn't you tell me?"

"Your dad wouldn't let me talk."

A while later, the oven's timer went off. Alyssa's mouth watered.

"The steak and potatoes are done." Mrs. Wilson said. "Jasmine, can you make the salad, please?"

"Yes, Mom." Jasmine took out a salad bag and balsamic vinaigrette dressing from the refrigerator and put them on the counter. She pulled her long waves into a high ponytail and poured the salad mix into a bowl.

"So how are you guys?" Jasmine asked Hailey and Alyssa.

"Okay," Alyssa said. "What about you?"

"Excited. This weekend, I'm performing in a horse show and getting my *Narnia* poster in the mail."

"Did you also hear about the storm tonight?" asked Alyssa.

Jasmine paused and turned to Alyssa. "There's a storm tonight?"

"Yeah," said Alyssa. "It's even supposed to knock out the power."

"What?" shrieked Leon, who sat next to Hailey.

"Leon, we have a generator," Jasmine said.

"Yes, but it only lasts for a little bit," said Leon.

"Well, Leon, be thankful that it'll be like having power," said Mrs. Wilson.

She carried a bowl of roasted potatoes and a plate of steak, while Jasmine carried the salad. Everyone helped him- or herself with each choice and ate.

"So, Jasmine and Leon, you guys had no idea about the storm tonight?" Mrs. Wilson asked.

The two shook their heads.

"It's supposed to sleet," said Mrs. Wilson.

"What's sleet?" asked Leon.

"Rain mixed with ice and snow," answered Mrs. Wilson.

"But the first day of spring is tomorrow," Leon said.

"It has snowed in April before," Jasmine said. "Plus, nothing really blooms here on the first day of spring anyway."

After dinner, a howl of wind loudened. Everybody turned to the closest window. Alyssa opened her mouth. Round yellow, green, and purple ice glowed and fell from the sky. The sleet hit the nearest window. Everyone ran to the window and stared at the sleet as it piled up on the ground.

"Why are the sleet funny colors?" Leon asked.

"Yeah, something's not right about this," said Jasmine.

Alyssa stayed silent. She didn't want to scare the Wilsons by revealing sorcery's existence.

"Alyssa, tell them what's going on," said Hailey.

"Why?" asked Alyssa.

"Just do it," Hailey said.

Alyssa sighed and turned to the Wilsons.

"Do you want to tell us something, Alyssa?" asked Mrs. Wilson.

"Um . . ."

"Why isn't the sleet white?" asked Leon.

"The truth's going to shock you," said Alyssa.

"Can you just tell us?" asked Jasmine.

"It's . . . magic."

All three gaped at her and stiffened their bodies.

"I thought there was no such thing as magic," said Leon.

"Well, the weather can't just change the color of sleet like that." Mrs. Wilson gazed out the window. "But I don't understand—why didn't we know about magic before?"

"I don't know." Alyssa shrugged.

Her mind shifted to Uncle Bruce. She felt her stomach harden and hurt. Her heart hammered, and breaths hurried out of her mouth. Anything could happen to him tomorrow morning. He could run away, abandoning her and Hailey. He could also turn evil, and then Alyssa might as well run away herself. Maybe he'd fall into a coma.

Well, whatever happened to him, it would harm her life. Hailey could call her grandparents to look after them.

If the power went out tonight and the roads had a lot of ice, then she and Hailey would likely still have no electricity tomorrow. Speaking of that, it went out.

"Mommy, when's the generator going to go on?" asked Leon.

"In a few seconds, sweetie," answered Mrs. Wilson. "It takes a little time before—"

The lights came back on, and there was a buzz.

"Is that the generator?" asked Alyssa.

"Yep," said Jasmine. "So—would you and Hailey like to go up to my room?"

"Sure," said Alyssa.

The girls headed up to Jasmine's room. The pale-blue wall had been covered with various basketball and horseback-riding ribbons and photos. Alyssa also noticed a giant *Harry Potter* movie poster next to Jasmine's bed as well as a bookshelf of fantasy books and movies. Now Jasmine would receive a *Narnia* poster.

Alyssa sighed at the room decor but formed a small grin. "Wow, nice room."

"Thanks," said Jasmine. "So I have some board games, cards, movies, crafts—what do you want to do while you're here?"

"My uncle's coming soon," said Alyssa. "So I don't think we can watch movies or do crafts."

"You still want to play cards or games?" asked Jasmine.

"Okay," said Alyssa.

"What do you have?" asked Hailey.

Jasmine listed the games and cards she had.

"We'll play Apples to Apples," Hailey said.

"Okay," said Jasmine. "Alyssa, does that sound good?"

"Yeah," said Alyssa.

Jasmine pulled the Apples to Apples box down from the top of her closet. "Oh, wait, that's for four players."

But a loud hissing occurred. Alyssa, Hailey, and Jasmine turned to the window as the noise grew louder. Alyssa's guts twisted. She heard her heart jackhammering.

"You'll be mine this weekend, Alyssa McCarthy," a deep French-accented voice said.

Alyssa gasped. The other two turned to her.

"Alyssa, what's going on?" asked Jasmine.

"Uh . . ."

"It sounds like someone's coming after you," Hailey said.

"About that—"

"Alyssa, just tell us what the heck is going on," said Jasmine.

"All right, someone *is* coming after me," said Alyssa. She turned to Hailey. "Remember that guy I told you about after I got that note?"

"The one responsible for—"

"Yes," said Alyssa. "He's kind of hunting for me."

Jasmine and Hailey inhaled.

"I better go tell my mom," said Jasmine.

Alyssa and Hailey followed Jasmine down the stairs. "Mom, someone's hunting Alyssa down! I heard his voice in my room!"

The three entered the kitchen, where Mrs. Wilson washed dishes. Mrs. Wilson turned to Jasmine, bending her eyebrows.

"No, I'm serious!" Jasmine squealed. "We all heard the voice in my room and—"

"What voice?" asked Mrs. Wilson.

Jasmine sighed. "There was a voice saying—"

"I didn't hear any voice, Jasmine," said Mrs. Wilson.

"There *was* one," said Alyssa.

"Yeah, someone said he wanted Alyssa this weekend," Hailey said.

"I don't know what you heard, but I didn't hear anything," said Mrs. Wilson.

"Mom, how could you have not heard the voice?" shrieked Jasmine.

"There was no voice." Leon stepped down the stairs.

"How is it that only Jasmine, Hailey, and I heard the voice?" asked Alyssa.

The doorbell rang, and Mrs. Wilson answered it. Uncle Bruce stood outside, holding an umbrella.

"Hey, Bruce," said Mrs. Wilson.

"Hello," said Uncle Bruce. He turned to Hailey and Alyssa. "Are you ready to go, girls?"

"Yeah," said Hailey.

"Uncle Bruce, did you hear a voice say my name?" Alyssa asked. "It was loud, so—"

Uncle Bruce tilted his head. "What are you talking about?"

"You didn't hear it, either, Mr. Flynn?" asked Jasmine.

"No. All I heard was the radio in my car."

"Oh my god, how did no one else hear it?" asked Alyssa.

"I don't know what you heard, Alyssa, but now's not the time to discuss it," said Uncle Bruce. "We need to get home safely. In fact, it'll take us longer since the roads have gotten icy."

He thanked the Wilsons and led Alyssa and Hailey into his car. Alyssa didn't understand how the voice could only be heard in Jasmine's room.

"Uncle Bruce, did you get the note?" Alyssa asked.

"F-from that Simon g-guy?"

"Yes," said Alyssa.

"Who the heck is he?" Uncle Bruce's teeth chattered.

"That was the marble figure I talked to. Did you see his note appear?"

"Right when I arrived here. I-I thought I was going to get a heart attack—that paper appearing on the passenger seat? I..."

"Did he at least tell you anything important?" Alyssa asked.

"H-he told me about those incidents, but he also told me about someone hunting for you and the storm harming me in some way."

"What's going to happen?" asked Hailey.

"He didn't say," said Uncle Bruce. "But . . . I'm really worried. I don't want anything to happen to me or you two. However, Hailey, you can call your grandparents once we get home. I'll let you use my cell phone."

"Thanks, Dad," said Hailey.

"Your punishment is also over because according to Simon, you weren't responsible for those incidents. He even proved it to me with a picture of a note. I didn't recognize the handwriting." Uncle Bruce sighed. "I'm sorry for not believing you."

Alyssa nodded and breathed. But her mind returned to what could happen to him tomorrow morning.

6

Last night the house had no power, and it had frozen enough that Alyssa had worn gloves, woolly socks, and a sweatshirt to bed. Waking up, Alyssa found sweat soaking her sweatshirt and feet. The heat must have come back on. Well, Alyssa's digital clock had lit up, so the power had returned.

Looking out the window, Alyssa saw sleet covering the neighborhood. But the sleet on the street shrank. Had it warmed up? In spite of what Jasmine had said last night about the first day of spring, temperatures could spike or plunge overnight.

The thought of Uncle Bruce and how he'd be harmed struck Alyssa's mind. Her stomach compressed. She hurried to his room. Cracking the door open, Alyssa gaped at him as he slept. Nothing seemed wrong. But he might reveal to her otherwise once he woke up.

Alyssa headed into the bathroom to do her routine and came back to Uncle Bruce's room. Her heart tap-danced against her chest. Chills rushed through her veins.

Uncle Bruce stretched and yawned. He looked at Alyssa and smiled. "Hi. Who are you?"

Alyssa gasped and ran out of Uncle Bruce's room. She banged on Hailey's door. "Hailey, get out here! Something bad has happened to your dad!"

"What?" Hailey opened the door.

"I . . . I think he lost his memory!" cried Alyssa.

"You think?" Hailey arched her eyebrows.

"No, sorry! He *definitely* lost his memory! He doesn't remember who I am!"

"Oh my god!" yelped Hailey.

Alyssa led her to Uncle Bruce's room. He still sat under the covers of his bed and grinned.

"I still haven't gotten your name," Uncle Bruce said to Alyssa.

"I'm Alyssa—your niece!"

"Who's the girl next to you?"

"Hailey—your daughter!"

"Okay, now who am I?"

"You're Bruce Flynn!" cried Hailey.

"Where am I?"

"Your room!" exclaimed Alyssa.

"Alyssa, we shouldn't just be answering his questions!" screeched Hailey. "We should call my grandparents!"

Alyssa followed her down the stairs.

"Why didn't you tell me my dad was going to lose his memory?" squealed Hailey.

"I didn't know! But isn't that why you're going to call your grandparents?"

"That's not the point, Alyssa!" growled Hailey. "You should've asked the marble figure!"

"He didn't know either!" Alyssa noticed tears flooding Hailey's eyes. "Hailey, please don't cry about this."

"Why?" choked Hailey. "I . . . I can't stand my dad like this." The tears streamed down her freckled cheeks.

"But you're going to call your grandparents," Alyssa said.

"You know what? *You* call them." Hailey wept.

Alyssa sighed and walked toward the phone. "Hailey, do you want to go wash your face?"

Hailey shook her head. "I'll watch you."

Alyssa took out the phonebook and looked up Hailey's grandparents' number. Then she dialed it and held the phone to her ear.

"Hello?" answered Donald, Hailey's grandpa. He'd invited Alyssa to call him that since she hadn't known what to address him as when she'd first met him several years ago.

"Hey, Donald, it's Alyssa."

Silence occurred for a few seconds. Donald said, "I haven't heard from you in a long time. What's been going on?"

"It's a long story. Listen, something just happened to Uncle Bruce, and we need your help."

"What happened?"

"He lost his memory."

Donald gasped. "H-how? Did he get into a bad car accident, or did something hit him on the head?"

"Neither."

"Then what wiped his memory?"

"Um . . . if I tell you, it may sound completely ridiculous."

"Just tell me."

"Okay—it was magic."

There was a pause. "Alyssa, don't say things like that. You sound stupid."

"But that's what it was. Nothing else could've wiped his memory overnight."

Donald sighed. "Okay."

"Anyway, can you and Kathleen come over, please?"

"Yes, but we can't come over now."

"Why not?"

"We went to Dover yesterday, and we're stuck in horrible traffic there, so we won't be able to come over for at least another three hours."

"Three hours?!"

"I'm sorry. But there's nothing I can do about it. If I could speed up traffic, I would."

Alyssa exhaled. "Fine. See you then." She hung up.

Hailey smeared the tears off her face and sniffled. Alyssa put her hand on her shoulder.

"Hailey, your grandparents are coming."

"Not for another three hours, though," croaked Hailey. "What are we going to do?"

Alyssa took her hand off Hailey's shoulder and stared into space. She couldn't send him to a special home for people who had brain or mental health issues now. That would probably take a while. She didn't know how many functions he'd lost nor did she have enough experience to take care of people with lower maturity levels or memory loss. She'd never even babysat, and she barely had any experience with babies and small children.

"We're going to have to wait until your grandparents come," said Alyssa. But she paused. "Wait—let's look up some ideas for what to do with your dad."

"But the study door's still locked," Hailey said. "I saw a combination lock on it last night."

"We'll take his phone," Alyssa said. "It has Internet."

The girls headed back upstairs and creaked Uncle Bruce's door open. He slept again.

"All right, I'll take his phone," whispered Hailey.

She tiptoed into his bedroom and aimed for his nightstand. The phone rested in its charger. She took it out and walked back toward Alyssa. Alyssa shut the door, and Hailey pressed the browser icon.

But the telephone ringing distracted Alyssa and Hailey. The girls raced each other down the stairs to answer it.

Alyssa picked it up. "Hello?"

"Hi, Alyssa," said Madison.

"Do you have power?"

"Yes. How do you still have phone cable?"

"Um . . . maybe Orion Street still has it. I don't know."

"Lucky. So are you able to come over today?"

"Uh . . . I don't know. Something happened to my uncle."

"What?"

"He lost his memory."

"What the heck?! How?!"

"It's complicated. But I don't know what to do with him."

"Come over and talk to my parents."

"Why can't I just—"

"They're making breakfast. My parents don't like having long conversations on the phone during meals."

"Let me ask Hailey." Alyssa turned to her. "Madison's inviting me over for breakfast."

"You're going to go?" asked Hailey.

"Madison said that her parents will talk to us about your dad."

"Why can't you call them?"

Alyssa told her why.

"Let me check to see if he's still sleeping first." Hailey referred to Uncle Bruce.

"All right. Do you want to come?"

"If my dad's okay."

Alyssa put the phone back to her ear. "Hailey's going to check on him."

"Cool," said Madison.

"So can you stay on the line, please?" asked Alyssa.

"Yes," said Madison.

After about a minute, Hailey returned. "He went back to sleep."

"You want to go?" asked Alyssa.

"Okay," said Hailey.

"We'll come," Alyssa told Madison.

"Cool. My house number is twenty-two. See you soon, Alyssa. Bye."

Alyssa hung up. She and Hailey got ready and stepped outside. The temperature had to be in the mid- to high fifties. The air warmed up enough that Alyssa had chosen to wear a half-sleeved button-down shirt and jeans but no coat for now. More snow continued to melt, but it still stood a few inches high. Good thing Alyssa and Hailey wore boots.

The fact that Hailey's grandparents wouldn't be able to come until later took over Alyssa's mind. What if Duchamp came before then? He could make himself invisible to anyone who could capture him, so even if someone called the police, it wouldn't do anything to help.

Approaching Draco Drive, Alyssa and Hailey looked for house number twenty-two. They passed a few homes until they found the Jennings's place. Alyssa rang the doorbell. Mrs. Jennings answered and looked around since her glasses had fogged up.

"Mrs. Jennings, we're in front of you." Alyssa waved.

Mrs. Jennings wiped her glasses on her apron and looked at Alyssa and Hailey. She smiled. "Hi, girls. Come in."

Alyssa and Hailey stepped inside.

"Mrs. Jennings, what are you cooking?" asked Hailey.

"Bacon and pancakes," she said. "Mr. Jennings also made scrambled eggs and sausages." She led them into the kitchen.

The smell of bacon drifted into Alyssa's nostrils. Her mouth watered. Back at home, Uncle Bruce had only made plain oatmeal with protein powder, egg whites and spinach, hard-boiled eggs, and fruit.

Mr. Jennings worked on his laptop. His wild dark-brown curls faced Alyssa, Hailey, and Mrs. Jennings.

"Brian, look who's here," said Mrs. Jennings.

Mr. Jennings turned to Alyssa and Hailey, grinning. "Hello." He looked at Alyssa. "Alyssa, you've really grown."

Alyssa giggled. "Thanks, Mr. Jennings, although I'm actually not that tall for my age."

"Well, you're certainly much taller than you were two years ago," Mr. Jennings said.

"Yeah, I guess," said Alyssa. "Where's Madison?"

"Mom, I can't find my iPod!" Madison jogged down the stairs.

"Well, you better keep trying because this is the second iPod I bought you," said Mrs. Jennings. "If you lose this one, I'm not buying you another one."

"But do that later," said Mr. Jennings. "Hailey and Alyssa are here."

"Oh, hi." Madison headed into the kitchen.

"Tara, can you get Kaitlyn, please?" Mr. Jennings asked Mrs. Jennings.

Mrs. Jennings nodded and called Kaitlyn, Madison's nine-year-old sister. Kaitlyn rushed down the stairs and skipped into the kitchen to let her strawberry-blonde waves bounce against her elbows. Both Kaitlyn and Madison had ADD, although Kaitlyn had more hyperactivity. Madison used to have severe ADD too. Until the summer before fourth grade, when she and Alyssa had first become friends, she would get in trouble a lot, especially at school.

As the girls sat down, Mr. and Mrs. Jennings brought out plates, cups, napkins, and silverware. Then they brought the food, followed by milk, cranberry juice, and orange juice. Everybody helped him or herself with the food. Mrs. Jennings, who sat next to Kaitlyn, poured syrup onto her pancakes.

"Hey, I wanted to do it," said Kaitlyn.

"Too bad," said Mrs. Jennings.

"But Madison got to do it," Kaitlyn said.

"Well, until you learn to control how much syrup you put on, I'm pouring it for you," said Mrs. Jennings.

Kaitlyn groaned.

"Kaitlyn Faye Jennings, if you complain, I'm taking your pancakes," Mrs. Jennings said.

Kaitlyn sighed, piercing the pancakes with her fork.

"Alyssa, your uncle actually l-lost his memory?" whimpered Madison.

"Yes." Alyssa nodded.

The Jennings family gasped.

"How?" asked Mr. Jennings.

"Uh . . . the truth's going to sound weird," said Alyssa.

"Tell us anyway." Mrs. Jennings loosened her sleek honey-blonde bun to let her hair fall past her shoulders. "The same thing happened to my dad when I was twenty-five."

"What happened?" Hailey asked.

Mrs. Jennings sighed. "He had mercury poisoning."

"Is that what your uncle got?" Kaitlyn asked.

"No . . . magic wiped his memories." Alyssa blushed.

Kaitlyn, Madison, and their parents pressed their lips, looking at Alyssa as if she'd spoken pig Latin.

"There's no such thing as magic," said Kaitlyn.

"Actually, there is," said Alyssa. "He lost his memory overnight."

"Yeah, he was completely fine yesterday," Hailey said. "Nothing hit him or anything."

"Remember the funny colors of the sleet last night?" asked Alyssa.

"Yeah," said Madison.

"Sleet is only supposed to be white," Mrs. Jennings said. "So that means . . ."

"Magic is real," said Alyssa.

The Jennings family gasped.

"I don't believe it," said Mr. Jennings.

"So, Alyssa, here's what you should do with your uncle," said Mrs. Jennings. "Do you have any other adult relatives?"

"We have my grandparents," Hailey said. "They're coming at one."

"Okay, Hailey, when they come, let them look for a doctor to check on him. Take him to the hospital and then find an assisted living home for him," Mrs. Jennings said. "But keep in mind that the homes won't just take him today. The process will take some time."

"How long?" Hailey asked.

"It depends on what rooms are available, when someone can interview your grandparents, and more importantly—if the home is available," said Mrs. Jennings. "It took my family ten days to get my dad into one after he got discharged from the hospital."

"Thanks." Hailey smiled.

"Thank you," said Alyssa.

"You're welcome," said Mrs. Jennings.

After breakfast, Alyssa and Hailey thanked the Jennings family and left. Alyssa hoped that Duchamp would not be there when she got home.

7

Alyssa and Hailey approached their house. But they jumped back. An engine roared from the backyard. It resembled—a helicopter? What would that do in a neighborhood? The engine even grew louder as Alyssa and Hailey drew nearer to their home.

They reached the house, and the same noise shook Alyssa's eardrums. She and Hailey turned to the backyard where the sound came from. The two walked toward it, but Alyssa clenched her teeth. Neither this area nor the property behind it had anything different.

The engine died out, but Alyssa and Hailey still looked around to see where the helicopter was. Alyssa saw nothing but sleet as well as everything she always saw.

"What's going on?" asked Hailey.

"I don't know."

"Why can't we see anything?"

"I think something's happening."

"Oh no."

"Let's go inside." Alyssa opened the backdoor and followed Hailey inside.

They walked down the hallway to the area by the front door—only for a strange voice with a French accent to say, "Bonjour, mesdemoiselles."

Turning to the kitchen, Alyssa and Hailey shrieked at the strange man. He stood only a few inches taller than Alyssa, despite his beach-ball-sized belly. The top of his bald head shone, and wild black hair surrounded it. A bushy mustache covered the area between his nose and upper lip. Yellow teeth filled his smile.

"Hello?" called Uncle Bruce. "Who's there?"

Everyone turned to him as he ran down the stairs. But the stranger held out his hand and made a stick appear. He pointed it at Uncle Bruce. "*Somnum harena!*"

Orange sand swirled out of the stick and found its way into Uncle Bruce's eyes. He cried out in pain and fell to the floor.

"Dad!" exclaimed Hailey.

"Silence!" The man pointed his stick at Hailey. "He won't wake up for another twelve hours."

Alyssa and Hailey gritted their teeth and whined. That stick he'd used to knock Uncle Bruce out had to be his wand. So this man had to be none other than . . .

"B-Beau Duchamp?" Alyssa asked.

"Yes," he said, "although I'd prefer Master Beau, if you don't mind."

"Never mind, what did you do to my dad?" yelled Hailey.

"I made him fall asleep," said Master Beau.

"You what?" Hailey stomped.

"Get out of here!" yelled Alyssa.

"No!" bellowed Master Beau. "I did all that stuff to harm you because I need you to have *zero* protections. That way, I can take you to the Fiji Islands as soon as possible."

"Well, I'm going to go get my dad's cell phone and call the police," said Hailey.

"No, you're not!" Master Beau pointed his wand at her.

"Stop it, Master Beau!" screamed Alyssa.

"*Somnum harena!*" he cast a spell on Hailey and knocked her out too.

Alyssa stood, speeding up her inhalations through her tensed chest. What else could Master Beau do?

"You've got to get out of here!" screeched Alyssa. "You're really—"

"Shut up!" Master Beau pointed his wand at her. "I'm going to do something to you that'll make you stop out!"

"What?"

Master Beau grinned. Alyssa backed away, sucking in breaths through her compressed teeth. She thought about what he might do, but Master Beau waved his wand and whipped it. He shot out a red ray of light. Alyssa screamed and turned around. But the beam hit her. What would it do now?

The answer wasn't to make her fall asleep, weaken her, or wipe her memory. But it did affect her brain. She felt distrust to Master Beau fading, and she now wanted to obey all his commands. Temptations to leave Hailey and Uncle Bruce took over her mind. Thoughts about hurting anyone trying to save her dominated as well.

"Well, Alyssa, how do you feel?" asked Master Beau.

Alyssa smiled and nodded. "Great."

"Look at yourself." Master Beau created a translucent mirror with his wand. Alyssa's pupils had turned red.

"Cool," said Alyssa.

"Now let's get you all packed up," said Master Beau.

He kicked Uncle Bruce out of the way and led Alyssa up the stairs. She then took him into her room and looked around for her suitcase. Where could it be? What color was it? Looking at the top shelf in her closet, Alyssa saw something large and red. Was that her suitcase?

"Hey, Master Beau, can you bring that bag down for me?" Alyssa asked. "I'm pretty sure it's my suitcase."

"Sure."

Master Beau pointed to the top of the closet and projected a pulling force onto the object. As he revealed the object, Alyssa saw wheels, pockets, and handles on it. Yup, it was her suitcase. Now she grabbed her old backpack from school.

Master Beau lowered the suitcase onto the floor and continued to hold out his wand. He pointed it toward the dressers.

Alyssa gazed at the electric-green spark at the tip of Master Beau's wand. Master Beau spun around, keeping that glimmer in the same spot.

He stopped moving. "All right, I've put all your clothes into your suitcase."

"You did?"

"Open it up."

Alyssa lifted the luggage cover and saw everything inside: shirts, pants, shorts—you name it. Then she gathered all her toiletries, some of her books and crafts, and shoes to put into her bags. She didn't have to worry about liquids in her backpack; she wasn't going to the airport.

Master Beau led her outside into the backyard. He pointed his wand to the center and whipped it around. Transparent colors formed and grew bolder by the second. A familiar shape formed, and Alyssa paid attention. Master Beau had created a helicopter.

"Whoa," Alyssa said.

"This is my own helicopter that I bought a few months ago," said Master Beau. "It even runs on magic and never runs out of it."

"Cool. But why was it invisible before?"

"So no one could see me, of course."

"Oh, right."

He carried Alyssa's suitcase as she climbed the ladder to the inside. She sat down and watched Master Beau point his wand at her suitcase. It unsolidified, thinning until it zoomed into the overhead compartment.

Alyssa placed her backpack under her seat and put her seatbelt on. Master Beau hopped into the pilot's seat. He started the engine, and the helicopter lifted. But . . . sparkles surrounded Alyssa's face. Her chest stung, and her muscles tightened. Looking out the window, she gasped. "Oh my god, what have I done?"

Her pupils had returned to black. She whimpered and whined. Her heart jackhammered inside her pained chest. Her mouth dried up. Breaths hurried out of her narrowed throat. Her toes and fingers tingled through her trembling hands and feet. Sweat spread throughout her entire body. Her stomach inflamed. She wanted to escape—or else she'd suffer . . . or die.

Master Beau turned to her, scowling and breathing through his gritted teeth.

"You monster!" Alyssa screamed. "You mean old monster!"

"Shut up!" he roared.

"How dare you put me under a spell!"

"I would do it again, except that those spells only work on people once in their lifetimes." He shook his head. "I can't believe the spell broke."

"Go back to my house!"

"Absolutely not!"

"Please! I . . . I'm going to die if you don't!"

"No! I don't have time for crybabies, so be quiet! We are going straight to the Fiji Islands, and that's final!"

"But—"

"Enough! I can't keep this stupid helicopter on autopilot just because you had a panic attack!"

"But I want to go home!" squeaked Alyssa as tears watered her eyes.

She buried her face into her hands and sobbed. Her life couldn't change. She couldn't leave home forever. Thoughts of her friends, Hailey, Uncle Bruce, Kathleen, Donald, and even Alex wandered in her mind. How would Kathleen and Donald react to her absence, the power outage, and Hailey and Uncle Bruce sleeping? Without her, they'd freak out. She refused to imagine how much.

About a few hours had passed since Master Beau kidnapped Alyssa. She'd fallen asleep after crying for a long time. She opened her eyes and stretched. But she clapped her hands over her mouth. Magenta smoke swirled in front of the helicopter. Oh no. Master Beau wouldn't fly into it, right?

"Okay, Alyssa, we're about to go into that portal over there," he said. "It'll take us straight to Fiji. We'll be going to this island called Yanowic. It's inhabited by wizards."

"What?" cried Alyssa.

"You heard. Once we get through, it'll be Monday, March 22nd, at four-thirty a.m."

"No, don't—"

"Shut up! For the last time, we are *not* going back!"

And his words seemed to have meant it. The helicopter touched the smoke and entered it. The blue of the sky faded as the pink took over. Dizziness tingled Alyssa's head and body as she watched the gas circle around her.

Her muscles tightened. Her heartbeats loudened in her chest, wrists, and forehead. She felt like bees had stung her stomach and created sharp pain. Within seconds, she'd be on the other side of the world.

A blue atmosphere revealed itself, erasing the smoky portal. Here it came—the Fiji Islands. The portal even shrank. Alyssa turned to the front; no way would she want to keep watching the swirl decrease in size.

Master Beau lowered the helicopter. Alyssa gazed out the window and eyed the cyan-colored Pacific Ocean, which splashed waves onto the whitish-beige beach. Palm trees stood tall, shadowing parts of the shore. But Master Beau turned away from it. Even if he landed there, Alyssa couldn't flee. A boat wouldn't even come to stop for her and take her home— not unless she had a parent or guardian with her as well as thousands of dollars.

Master Beau soared over a forest. Alyssa watched the helicopter descend. It landed near a building. What could be inside it, and what would Master Beau do to her there?

"Okay, Alyssa, time to get out." Master Beau turned off the engine.

"No," she said.

Master Beau disappeared and then appeared outside Alyssa's door. He blasted it open with his wand and glared at her. "You do not refuse anything I demand! So either you get out, or I fill the helicopter with water while you're locked inside!"

Alyssa opened her mouth and leaned back. She had never heard anyone threaten her with that level of danger. Wait—maybe there'd be a way to escape once Master Beau was busy. She stood up, though, and pulled her backpack from underneath her seat.

"Leave everything behind. You can take them later."

"But—"

"Do as you're told, McCarthy!" Master Beau grasped her wrist and lead her to the building. She might as well scream at it.

Strands of barbed wire surrounded the dark-gray stone building, creating a fence with prickly wires that could hurt someone. A giant black banner with a skull and crossbones in the center had been spread across the front of the building. The chimney let out black smoke in the shapes of skulls and even hissing serpents.

"I . . . I'm not going in there," Alyssa said, her voice shaking.

"Yes, you are. Don't be a baby. I wouldn't bring you here for vacation."

Alyssa remained silent.

"Let's go!" Master Beau pulled Alyssa to another part of the fence. He pointed his wand at it, causing the strands of wire to drop. Then he and Alyssa walked inside, heading toward the front door. Alyssa's chest stung as Master Beau opened the door and pulled her inside.

8

What happened behind the glass in the dimly lit hallway made Alyssa gasp. Men and women tested dark magic on rats, tarantulas, toads, and hermit crabs. Some rats had glowing-red eyes, which hinted to Alyssa that they had been put under spells. The red-eyed rats drank potions, giving them warts or suffocating them. Tarantulas flew in different directions based on those in which the testers' wands pointed them. Toads squealed and cried loud enough that Alyssa could hear them as they experienced pain and torture. Hermit crabs turned into stone or flew back onto the counters and broke their shells.

Behind each counter floated computer monitors, scanning the workers' progress from failure to success, with poor, satisfactory, and good in between. Most of them succeeded with their testing, according to the screens.

How obnoxious and disgusting, though! Alyssa had always hated animal testing, but this exceeded anything she'd ever seen before. Tears stung her eyes from that.

"All right there, Master Beau?" said a bald man with a British accent as he left the hallway from his right.

Alyssa turned to him.

"Hey, David," said Master Beau.

"Are you sure you want just one child?" David asked.

"What do you mean?" asked Master Beau.

"Weakening and killing one child will not make you powerful enough to rule all of France," David said.

"Where'd you find that out?" Master Beau asked.

"I hacked into a blocked Magic Carpet World Connections site about abusing dark magic and becoming an evil dictator," said David. "It said that no wizard, no matter how powerful they are, can rule one country with weakening only one child who has a magical connection with him or her—unless it's a small country."

"So what I heard a few years ago was wrong?" asked Master Beau.

"Not at the time. The website also said that someone in the International Magic Control changed the satellite last week after another evil wizard ruled all of Vivanesia."

"Not too far from here," said Master Beau.

"You'll need at least four or five children to make connections with," said David. "That person in the IMC actually meant to block it, but it didn't work, unlike the killing and memory-wiping spells."

"Well, that's good," said Master Beau. "But where can I find more kids?"

"I'll try to hack into another website as soon as I can to find out about that," said David. "There's also a new way to make connections overnight at most, so now you don't have to wait several months. I'll look into that for you too."

"Really?" asked Master Beau.

"Yep," said David.

"Thank you," said Master Beau.

"You're welcome." David walked back down the hallway direction from where he'd come from.

"All right, Alyssa, up to the prison room," said Master Beau.

"No," she said.

Footsteps thumped. The two turned to the sound. It grew louder, but Alyssa saw no one.

"Hello?" asked Master Beau. "Who's there?"

A pointed tip stuck out and spun. It let out a light-blue ray that hit Master Beau. Alyssa watched his pupils glow blue.

"Alyssa, I shouldn't be doing this," Master Beau said.

She lifted her eyebrows. Master Beau must have gone under a spell.

"You're going to let me go?"

"Yes. Go and find someone to take you back home."

"Okay, thanks." Alyssa turned to the wand that stuck out of the air while Master Beau ran away in tears. The air peeled itself and revealed a strange woman. Alyssa gasped.

"Sorry." The woman slid her sheer hood off.

"What are you wearing?" asked Alyssa.

"An invisibility poncho. I snuck in here and put Master Beau under a spell to save you."

"Thank you."

"You're welcome, but *please* don't tell anyone I did that. It's illegal. Master Beau, his workers, and this building have charms around them to—"

"I know—to protect them from the police and government."

"How'd you know?"

"A marble figure told me."

"Let's talk after we get out of here." The woman stepped out of her poncho.

But Alyssa stood and remained mute.

"You need to trust me."

"You . . . you're trying to help me?"

"Yes. So do you trust me?"

Alyssa stayed silent.

"Do you?"

Alyssa swallowed and showed gritted teeth. "Uh . . . yeah."

"Then let's go."

Alyssa followed her outside. The lady whipped her wand and broke the entrance wires. She led Alyssa out of the center.

"Was the marble figure you mentioned the same one I saw?" the woman flicked her waist-length golden hair behind her shoulders.

"Did he have a British accent?"

"Yes. He told me where to find you."

"That was the one who told me about Master Beau. His name's Simon."

"I think that's the one who signaled me. So anyway, I'm Isabelle Cunningham."

"Hi, Ms. Cun—"

"Call me Isabelle."

"I'm Alyssa, Alyssa McCarthy."

"Yup. Simon told me your name and what you looked like."

"Wow." Alyssa turned to the helicopter. "My stuff is still in there. You don't mind getting it, do you?"

"Not at all." Isabelle led Alyssa to the helicopter. "I'm going to suck your suitcase out." She held out her hand and made her wand appear. Then she pointed it to the helicopter.

The colors crashed onto the ground and piled up on one another like the computer-generated molecules Alyssa had watched in science during school. Alyssa noticed that the colors also turned red, and only that same shade came out and covered the other colors like wrapping paper. The tones in some areas darkened into black. Those shrunk and thinned on top of the red. They became the handles, wheels, and zippers. Isabelle repeated that effect for Alyssa's backpack and let the hues and textures stiffen.

"Whoa." Alyssa picked up her suitcase handles and followed Isabelle. Isabelle pointed her wand out. Alyssa gaped and observed the wand's position. What would Isabelle need to cast if nothing besides trees, rocks, and plant life stood in this forest?

The two stopped. Isabelle tilted her wand up. Colors solidified into something the size of a helicopter. The top rounded and had a window covering the front half. The bottom was whitish silver and had no wings or even a rotor. It probably had to rely on magic for power. Then maybe it didn't need wings or a rotor. It did look like a flying jet that some cartoons had used to portray for the ideal future.

"Isabelle, what is that?" Alyssa asked.

"This is my flying tube. Let's hop in before anything happens."

Alyssa climbed into the back, and Isabelle sucked her bags into the overhead bin. Isabelle hopped into the pilot's seat and pressed a blue button that turned on the engine. She held onto two handles and allowed the tube to ascend.

"Isabelle, where are we going?"

"We're going to a more deserted part of Yanowic. We need to be safe from the dark wizards."

"Will I be able to go home?"

"Perhaps."

"Really?"

"I have a private pilot that might be able to do it. In wizarding culture, you can have private pilots."

"Cool."

"But I have to see if he's available first."

"Thanks, Isabelle."

The two took off and flew over the forest. Alyssa looked out the window. *I wonder where she's taking me.*

A couple minutes had passed, and the beach came closer. Isabelle pressed an orange button. The tube lowered by a few feet and steadied down its descent until it reached the ground. Isabelle turned off the engine. She and Alyssa hopped out of the tube.

Isabelle pointed her wand at the vehicle and dissolved the colors. The pigments blended into the air and faded.

"Wow!" Alyssa whispered.

"I know—it's really cool. So let me get my cell phone."

She pointed her wand to her other hand and created what looked like an iPhone. Alyssa grinned. "Is that an iPhone?"

"It's actually a *Wi*Phone, Alyssa." Isabelle laughed. "Just like you have Apple, we wizards have Watercress. But the WiPhone is the magical equivalent to the iPhone."

"Wow, so you have WiPods too?"

"Mm-hm. Anyway, let me call the pilot."

But a swish occurred. Isabelle and Alyssa turned to a frowning man with tannish-brown skin and a short afro. "Isabelle, are you trying to call your pilot?"

"Yes, Mathias." Isabelle turned to Alyssa. "Alyssa, this is my boyfriend, Mathias."

"Hi." Alyssa waved.

"Hello, Alyssa," said Mathias. "I have some bad news for you."

"What is it?"

"You're unable to leave the country," said Mathias.

Alyssa stretched her jaw. She'd thought she had gone so close to returning home. One phone call would have led her back to New Jersey.

"You're kidding," said Alyssa.

"No, I'm not," Mathias shook his head. "Master Beau and his workers have created an invisible wall about twenty-five miles out. It's all around the border of the country."

"When did he do this?" asked Alyssa.

"I just came back from the dark magic center where I overheard two of his workers saying that he'd done it as soon as you and he entered this country," said Mathias.

"What were you doing there?" asked Isabelle.

"You texted me saying that you were putting Master Beau under a spell," said Mathias. "I went to see if he was still under it, but when I got there, he was back to normal."

"What'll happen if I try to leave?" Alyssa asked.

"You'll bump into the wall," said Mathias. "Master Beau will only take it down if he succeeds in killing you and is ready to rule France."

"So you mean—I'm stuck here?"

"I'm afraid so," Mathias nodded. "Until Master Beau dies or we find a way to break the wall, you won't be able to go home."

Alyssa sighed and walked away from Mathias and Isabelle. She sat, and tears watered her eyes. She smeared them with the back of her hand. There had to be a way to break the wall. Hailey,

Kathleen, and Donald must already cry and wonder where Alyssa had gone.

Footsteps splashed onto the sand. Mathias and Isabelle ran up to Alyssa, and she deepened her breathing and wiped her eyes.

"Alyssa, you don't need to get upset," said Isabelle. "We'll find a way to either break the wall or defeat Master Beau."

"What is it going to be?" choked Alyssa.

"I don't know," said Isabelle. "We'll find something."

"Hello, folks," said Simon.

Everyone turned around. Simon flew toward them. Alyssa noticed that he wore a T-shirt and shorts instead of a suit. Everybody greeted him, and Isabelle and Mathias introduced themselves.

"How'd you change your clothes, Simon?" asked Alyssa.

"Marble figures can change their outfits like humans," Simon said. "They attach to our bodies after wearing them for a few minutes." He turned to Mathias and Isabelle. "Anyway, I came here to ask you guys if you could be Alyssa's mentors. Have you heard about Master Beau closing—"

"Yes." Mathias nodded.

"We'll be her mentors," said Isabelle.

"Brilliant," said Simon. "Isabelle, do you have something to shelter us?"

Isabelle nodded and pulled out a tiny object from her tube. It looked like a beanbag.

"Isabelle, how are you going to—"

"You'll see, Alyssa." Isabelle ran with the object and placed it down. Then she held out her wand and directed it at the object. "*Inflet tabernaculum.*"

The bag swelled, expanding like a bag of popcorn in a microwave. It doubled in size—and then it tripled. And before Alyssa knew it . . . *pop!* A tent appeared. Alyssa's smile shrank. The tent stood shorter than her and had no platform at the bottom.

"Come on, Alyssa." Isabelle waved toward herself.

"You've got to see the inside of Isabelle's tent." Mathias clapped his hand onto Alyssa's shoulder.

"Why?" she asked.

"It's not your average tent," said Mathias.

"What's inside?" Alyssa asked.

"You'll see," said Isabelle.

9

Alyssa opened the flap and lowered her jaw. A staircase revealed itself, and Isabelle turned on the lights from beneath. What lay beneath the ground?

Burnt orange filled the walls. Tan carpet textured the floor of the room in which Alyssa stood, which was probably the living room. A thick copper rug with gold and dark green horizontal stripes covered the center. A caramel-colored coffee table stood on top of the rug. Two black leather couch chairs faced the widths of the rug and table. A wide couch faced Alyssa. Alyssa turned to the wall next to the kitchen and saw a plasma-screen TV attached to it.

She strolled into the kitchen. The color scheme transitioned into silver, black, and light blue. A marble island stood in the center, with black stools on one side and a silver sink in the center. Blue tiles decorated the floor. A glass booth table, surrounded by black leather chairs, took up the near left corner. A silver refrigerator lined up against the wall across from Alyssa. The stove and oven bordered it. A microwave hung above the stove. A toaster rested on the counter next to it. Cabinets covered a corner.

"I . . . I don't believe it," Alyssa said.

"It's all magic," said Isabelle. "So . . . you want to call your family and tell them you're okay?"

"Yes."

"Mathias, can you get Alyssa's stuff while she calls her family?" Isabelle asked.

Mathias nodded and jogged upstairs. Isabelle held out her hand, and her phone appeared into it. She tapped the back of it with her wand.

Alyssa tilted her head. "Isabelle, why are you tapping your phone?"

"It's how you charge it."

Alyssa clenched her lips.

"You have to think or say the right spell for it. All magical technology is wireless. Even TVs and lamps are like that."

"Wow, that's cool."

"We also don't have to deal with power outages or dead zones when it comes to phone calls," Isabelle added.

"Lucky."

"But the spell only works on magical technology. Anyway, why don't you call your family?" Isabelle gave the device to Alyssa. "Do you know how to dial on a touchscreen phone?"

"Well . . . I've borrowed some of my friends' phones to call my uncle. My uncle also let me use his phone to call people occasionally. But that was, like, a while ago."

"Do you want me to dial the number for you?"

Alyssa looked up.

"You could also say the full name and address of the person you want to call, and it'll connect to them."

"Okay."

Isabelle tapped her phone with her finger a couple of times and handed it to Alyssa.

"Say it now," she whispered.

"Call Hailey Elizabeth Flynn on Seven Orion Street, Bursnell, New Jersey." Alyssa put the phone up to her ear, listening to the ringing until the Flynns' voicemail came through. Right—twelve hours hadn't passed yet, so Hailey and Uncle Bruce wouldn't wake up.

Alyssa left a message. "Hi, Hailey and Uncle Bruce. It's Alyssa. That evil wizard has kidnapped me to the Fiji Islands, and I won't be able to come back until after he dies. But I am okay, and I hope you are too. I hope see you guys soon. I love you. Bye." Alyssa handed the phone back to Isabelle.

Mathias staggered down the stairs, carrying Alyssa's bags.

"Need some help, Mathias?" Alyssa asked.

"You want to carry your suitcase?" asked Mathias.

"Okay." Alyssa took her suitcase and stepped down the stairs. Isabelle led the two into the bedroom.

The carpet was beige. A chocolate-brown dresser faced everyone. Three double beds with gold-embroidered copper quilts lined up against the wall next to one another. Two sets of pillows covered the headboard. One set matched the quilt's colors, and the others had cotton material and a cream color. Two short amber nightstands stood between the three beds. A stout lamp stood on top of one nightstand.

"Oh my god," whispered Alyssa.

"Hello, guys," Simon appeared into the bedroom and held a touchscreen tablet.

"Don't tell me that's the new WiPad you're holding," said Mathias.

"No, of course not," said Simon. "That's not supposed to come out until the iPad does."

"When will that be?" Alyssa asked.

"April third," answered Simon. "This is called Triton's Tablet. It's one of the most advanced Microchant tablets right now." He turned to Alyssa. "Microchant is the wizarding version of Microsoft."

"Cool," said Alyssa.

"Where'd you buy that?" asked Mathias.

"The Microchant Store," said Simon. "Anyway, I rented a tracking app on it, which is only legal during emergencies. Once this is over, I'll have to return it."

"So that's how you're going to track down Master Beau?" Isabelle asked.

"Yup," said Simon. "It'll actually show me videos of what he's doing. There's a camera signal in the app."

"That's great." Isabelle nodded. "So does anyone want breakfast?"

Alyssa giggled. "I think it's lunchtime for me."

"Isabelle, why don't you give her the Chronocurrent potion?" asked Mathias.

"What's that?" Alyssa referred to the potion.

"It's a potion that adjusts your mind to the time zone you're in," said Mathias.

"So I won't be jetlagged after drinking it?"

"Nope," replied Mathias.

"I'll show you where it is," Isabelle said.

Alyssa followed her to the closet next to the bathroom. Cardboard boxes of small plastic bottles sat at the bottom. Alyssa noticed the liquids' various colors and textures. "Are these the potions, Isabelle?"

"Yup. My parents used to work in a potion store, and after they retired, they gave me all of their unsold potions."

"Neat," Alyssa said.

Isabelle bent down and pulled out a plastic bottle filled with a gooey white potion. Alyssa screwed up her face since that potion looked like glue.

"Okay, Alyssa, here you go." Isabelle handed it to her.

She took it, and her stomach twisted. Pressing her lips on the bottle spout, she let the liquid fall into her mouth. But a sugary sensation and creamy texture filled her mouth. The potion tasted like . . . vanilla.

After finishing the last bits, Alyssa removed the spout from her mouth and exhaled. "That was actually really good."

"I'm glad." Isabelle smiled. "Why don't you go throw that away?"

Alyssa nodded and tossed it into the kitchen garbage. Isabelle gave her water and gathered Mathias and Simon into the kitchen for breakfast. Alyssa's mind rewound into morning mode. Thoughts of drinking orange juice and eating eggs, bacon, and French toast meandered into her mind.

She told Isabelle what she wanted to eat. Instead of standing up, Isabelle remained sitting, pointing her wand at Alyssa's side of the table. Not only did the colors solidify, but the scents also grew stronger. Scents of the French toast and orange juice's sweetness as well as the bacon's aroma floated into Alyssa's nostrils.

Once the food had reached full solidity, Alyssa dug in. While she ate, Isabelle also created some porridge for Simon, an omelet for Mathias, and stuffed French toast for herself.

"I didn't know you could also create food with magic," said Alyssa. "It's too bad people like me can't do as much as wizards."

"We're actually not even supposed to expose magical cooking or technology to ordinary people," Isabelle said. "The wizarding government thinks that it can cause envy and even violence."

"But you showed it to me," Alyssa said.

"That's because you're only one person," said Isabelle. "But we couldn't advertise the WiPhone at a mall. And when you go home, please don't tell anyone about our technology."

"I won't," said Alyssa.

"Thank you," said Isabelle.

During breakfast, Alyssa had learned a lot about wizarding culture from Isabelle and Mathias. Before a wizard could learn magic, they had to let out uncontrollable magic at least three times, which normally started at six years old. Once a child turned nine, his or her parents could hire a tutor to teach the child magic at home. By the age of sixteen, a wizard was expected to know most kinds of magic, and by age eighteen, he or she was expected to know all that could be learned.

Young wizards aged nine to fifteen were forbidden to use magic outside of their homes at any time for any reason. They had too little experience and could cause harm without realizing. Wizards aged sixteen and seventeen could only perform magic outside of their homes under the supervision of adults over twenty-one. When wizards turned eighteen, they could use sorcery outside of their homes by themselves.

Alyssa changed into denim shorts and a U-neck olive shirt. She left the bathroom and strode over to Simon. "Simon, can we see what Master Beau is doing?"

"Sure." Simon took out his tablet and pressed it a few times.

Alyssa sat next to him and leaned toward the tablet screen. A light-blue background showed a dot with the name Beau Duchamp over it. Simon slid his finger from the side, which brought out a list of choices. He pressed View by Video, and a window popped up.

Master Beau stood in a gray room next to a desktop computer with no plug. He walked toward a wire attached to the system unit. The wire led to a suction cup, which led to a . . . snake. The snake had a gray body and a light-orange belly. It stayed still with its eyes shut.

A timer went off on the computer's monitor. Master Beau pressed a button on the keyboard, and it stopped. Someone knocked on the door.

"Come in," Master Beau said.

The door opened to reveal David.

"Is that the ash-breathing adder?"

"Yep. How'd you know?"

"I read a lot."

"Well, this is going to find Alyssa, that girl I captured, and kill her. And no matter where she goes or hides, it'll find her and bite her till she dies."

"Very well."

Master Beau took the suction cup off the snake. It opened its glimmering red eyes.

"You can go now," Master Beau said to it.

The snake nodded and disappeared.

Simon closed the app.

"I hate snakes," groaned Alyssa. Snakes had frightened her ever since she was little. Even in pet stores, she'd always avoided them.

"We can look up ways to defeat it," Isabelle told her.

"But the snake is impervious to wand and potion magic, like most magical creatures," said Simon.

"So then how is Master Beau—"

"He has something called a brain-domination computer, Mathias," said Simon. "That was what we saw. It's a computer that has a suction cup to hook up magical creatures to make them loyal to whoever bought the computer. That's the only exception for where they can't resist the magic. Isabelle and Mathias, I suggest you look up what the snake eats and what kills it. I don't want Alyssa near anything dangerous."

"Okay," said Isabelle.

After spending a few minutes on their MagBook Dragon and Pegasus (the magical equivalents to the MacBook Pro and Air), Isabelle and Mathias looked up at Alyssa, who watched them.

"Okay, what'd you find out?" Alyssa asked.

"The snake eats rainbow-patched white mice and gets killed by metallic fronds," said Isabelle.

"We'll find them in the rainforest," said Mathias.

"What are we going to keep the mice in though?" asked Isabelle.

"I have an old hamster cage in my house," Mathias said.

"You're going to use that?" Isabelle closed her laptop.

"Yeah," said Mathias. "It's still fine."

"How are you going to capture the mice?" Alyssa asked.

"There's a spell for it," Mathias stood up. "I'll be back, guys." He held out his arms and disappeared.

About a half hour had gone by, and footsteps thumped down the stairs. Alyssa figured out that Mathias had returned via his flying tube since Isabelle had said that he owned one too. Alyssa turned to the staircase and watched him carry a small cage with about six or seven mice. They had white fur with patches of green, purple, red, and blue. Mathias also carried a bag of silver, gold, copper, metallic green, red, and blue fronds.

He entered the living room and sat on one of the couch chairs. He placed the cage on the carpet. But Isabelle bent her eyebrows. "Mathias, don't put them on the carpet. They're going to—"

"Isabelle, it's okay. They're in a cage."

"Still, they're filthy wild animals, and they could get my clean carpet dirty."

"Oh, Isabelle, stop being such a neat freak," said Mathias.

"No." Isabelle turned to Simon, who sat on the other couch chair and listened to his WiPod. "Simon, can you track the snake, please?"

Simon took out his earbuds. "What did you want me track? I didn't get that."

Isabelle repeated herself, and Simon made his tablet appear. Alyssa watched him press it; he probably programmed a way to track the snake.

"Simon, how far away is the snake?" asked Alyssa.

"Erm . . . about a hundred feet away," he replied.

"Oh my god," moaned Alyssa.

"Let's go," said Isabelle.

Alyssa's stomach hardened as she walked up the stairs. She could even feel her heart throb through her throat. She hurried her breathing and followed everyone else out of the tent.

Alyssa stepped onto the sand and saw something move. She gasped, her muscles constricting to her bones. Her hands shook and cooled down despite the burning sun. Tingles spread through her toes and fingers and expanded to the rest of her body. She whined through her contracted throat. She wished that what she saw was just a mirage. But the smell of the ash hanging in the air revealed to her that she didn't just see things—the snake drew nearer.

It opened its jaw, exhaling light gray ash. It stuck out its pointy black tongue and pushed its head toward Alyssa, and she coughed. But it sped up its slithering. Alyssa screamed and spun around. She dashed along the beach, and her feet sped up, thus kicking the backs of her legs.

"Alyssa, get back here!" yelled Mathias. "I can't disappear holding the cage or mice! It's impossible doing both!"

But Alyssa continued to sprint across the beach. Sand streamed into her sneakers. Sweat even trickled into the neckline of her shirt and her legs.

Something scaly slapped her legs. She flew into the air and screamed. Her body fought against the direction of the breeze, and she landed on her butt.

She moaned and quickened up breaths through her gritted teeth. The snake continued to slither and release ash. Shrieking, Alyssa bolted up and turned around. She headed into the rainforest.

Facing vines, twigs, trees, bushes, and fronds, Alyssa found her way around them. Her legs ached from all the different movements she made. She ran sideways from a tree, jumped over a couple of twigs and vines, and zigzagged around trees and bushes. A trail even lay in front of her.

Alyssa's thin legs and body kept her energy going, but her legs felt like they'd been clogged with broken cobblestones. The snake kept chasing her, though.

Alyssa hastened down the trail, inhaling and exhaling. Her throat had dried up, making her cough along the way. The ash the snake breathed increased her coughing. She stopped but opened her eyes.

About seven or ten feet below her stood a brownish-green pond. A waterfall sound made her eyes drift to where it came from. It poured water into it and not far from where she stood.

Turning around, Alyssa saw the snake slither only a couple of feet away, sticking its tongue out at her. Gasping, she backed away, and her heel stepped off the cliff. The ball of her foot slid off too, and she screamed as she fell into the water.

She landed with a splash and sank into the freezing water while holding her breath. Kicking her feet, Alyssa struck toward the surface and fought the pressure.

Poking her head out of the water, Alyssa gasped. Water vapor clouded her face, revealing to her that she'd come close to the waterfall. Swimming away from it, Alyssa heard Isabelle and Mathias call her. Had they killed the snake?

Nope. The snake popped out of the water and breathed ash into Alyssa's face. She coughed and turned around, speeding up her crawl to swim faster.

"Alyssa, get over here!" bellowed Mathias.

Alyssa turned to where he and Isabelle stood on the shore and then went around the snake by going underwater and swimming away from it. She increased the speed of her kicking feet and the crawling of her arms. She felt the rocks with her hands under the water as she huffed. A flying movement from above her caught her attention. She saw a mouse and metallic frond coming to the water. The absence of water plopping hinted to her that the snake had eaten the creature.

Now that Alyssa reached an area with less depth, she placed her feet at the bottom and stood up. Turning to the snake, she saw it floating on its back and the remaining ash drifting away into the air. She coughed and panted. She struggled to walk with her aching, biting-cold legs, But the looks on Isabelle's and Mathias's faces made her want to punish herself.

"I . . . I'm sorry."

"What you did was very dangerous, Alyssa," Isabelle said. "You really could have been killed."

"I know," she said.

"We had to fly all the way here in the tube just to save you," Isabelle added. "It would've been a lot easier to feed the snake a mouse back on the beach and get it over with."

"I said I was sorry," said Alyssa. "But I told you that I had a bad fear of snakes."

"We understand that," said Mathias. "But you're going to have to learn to control yourself."

Alyssa sighed. "Okay."

"Now let's go back to set up the tent," said Isabelle.

Her tube had been parked by a tree at the shore's edge. The three strode over to it and hopped inside.

10

Last night Isabelle and Mathias had told Alyssa that no spell or potion could fight people's fears. Alyssa had considered how she could control her actions next time something threatening came. But Simon had checked his tablet last night and had revealed that Master Beau had hooked up zero creatures to his computer. Alyssa hoped that Simon would check again today, though.

She had just finished her morning routine in the bathroom and had dressed herself in khaki short shorts and a blue T-shirt. Simon howled with laughter from the bedroom, so Alyssa opened the door. Simon watched a slapstick comedy video on his Wizdreams laptop, a type of Microchant computer.

"Simon?" Alyssa asked.

"Yes?" Simon closed his video.

"Can we see what Master Beau is doing now?"

"Sure. Why don't you get Mathias and Isabelle too?"

Alyssa walked into the kitchen, where Isabelle and Mathias used their wands to make breakfast.

"Simon wants you guys," Alyssa said.

"What for?" asked Isabelle.

"To see what Master Beau is doing."

"Why don't you ask him to bring his tablet here?" asked Mathias.

"Okay." Alyssa turned to the bedroom. "Simon, do you mind bringing your tablet here?"

"Not at all." Simon held his device and flew out of the bedroom.

Alyssa ate her milk and cereal and observed Simon. He pressed a spy icon, which Alyssa assumed was the tracking app. She watched him do everything to get the video of what Master Beau did now. He sat with David in his office.

"Thank you for showing me the online article about the technique for making magical connections with people's genes," said Master Beau. "I had no idea that royal purple granite and curly black grass had that much magic to turn a complicated task into a simple one."

"You're never too old to learn," said David. "Another thing you need to know is that the other children you make connections with must be close to the girl's age."

"How close?"

"No more than two years. So while a fourteen-year-old kid would be eligible, a nine-year-old wouldn't."

"Where can I find them?"

"The website I read this on didn't say that. I'll have to hack into another one to find out. In the meantime, I'll go find and tranquilize another magical creature for your computer."

"Make sure it's big and vicious so that Alyssa can't defeat it."

Everyone gasped as Simon closed his app.

"Let's get ready to go now," said Isabelle. "I have everything we need."

"What are we going to do?" asked Alyssa.

"Destroy the computer," said Isabelle.

Alyssa followed Isabelle, Mathias, and Simon to the closet. Isabelle opened her closet and pulled out two plastic bottles. One had a potion that looked like Coke or Pepsi with its fizziness and dark color. The other one looked like apple cider with a light caramel-brown color.

"Are those potions sweet?" Alyssa asked.

"The Normalla potion, which is the light brown one, is a little bit, but the Impersonaide potion is sour," said Isabelle.

"Did you think they looked like apple cider and soda?" asked Mathias.

Alyssa nodded. "What do they do?"

"The Impersonaide potion turns you into someone else," said Isabelle.

Alyssa grimaced. "How?"

"You'll see," said Isabelle.

"What about the Normalla potion?" asked Alyssa.

"It undoes the Impersonaide potion's effects," replied Isabelle.

Alyssa nodded but gritted her teeth.

"I'm going to get the supplies." Isabelle turned back to the closet and leaned down. She gathered rubbing sticks, paper cups, sheer ponchos, and a small bag.

Everyone walked out of the tent, and then Isabelle shrank it back into its small object form.

"Mathias, you take Simon," said Isabelle. "I'll take Alyssa."

He nodded and led Simon to his flying tube. But a growl rumbled, and everybody stopped. The sound came from the bushes behind the palm trees. Alyssa turned to it and stared. The others gaped as well.

Iciness rushed through Alyssa's veins and chilled them as pointy white ears drew nearer. The ears darkened into tan and turned parallel to the bush.

"Not a color-changing dingo," mumbled Simon.

Alyssa unclenched her aching teeth and dropped her jaw. Her breaths quickened out of her mouth and dried it up. Her hands froze and shook, and the dingo growled again. Alyssa's eyes focused on its every movement. It halted and turned to her and her mentors. Its snout stuck out and growled, exposing its foamy yellow teeth. It walked out of the hedges, showed its head, and trotted.

"Everybody, run!" Mathias hustled, leading the others away from the dingo.

Alyssa sprinted and screamed, drying out her mouth more. The wind, however, blew in the opposite direction. She pushed herself against it and turned around. The dingo galloped and barked.

Isabelle shrieked, and Alyssa and Mathias halted. The dingo stuck its nails into Isabelle's leg. Mathias picked up a seashell and threw it at the creature. It pulled its nails out of Isabelle and looked at him. Isabelle lay motionless and produced no sounds.

Mathias turned around, but the dingo beat him and stabbed its nails into his leg. He fell forward and thumped onto the ground.

"Mathias!" Alyssa ran over to him and knelt down.

"Alyssa, save yourself!" exclaimed Simon. "I'll send a signal to someone to save you!"

"Just me?" yelled Alyssa.

But Simon shut his eyes and floated in the air. The dingo jumped up and bit his foot.

"Ow!" yelled Simon.

"Simon!"

The dingo continued to bite Simon, and it used its mouth to slam him on the ground. A marble chip broke off Simon's hair.

"No, no!" screeched Alyssa, tears filling her eyes. She knelt beside Simon, who lay with his eyes shut; he made no movements or sounds.

But a caw attracted Alyssa. She saw a creature the size of a horse. It had the head, wings, and front legs of a rainbow lorikeet.

The back half of its body, however, had the tail and legs of a kangaroo. The creature scratched its front legs against the back of the dingo, which whimpered and howled. But the fight between both animals turned Alyssa away. The dingo's sounds died out. Alyssa stood up and gazed at it as it lay dead. The birdlike creature turned to her.

"Thanks," Alyssa muttered.

The creature walked toward her and she backed away. But she noticed a large tag on its front right leg where the following words were spelled out:

Do not fear me. I am here to help you. My name is Regulus. I am a marshakeet, which is half lorikeet and half kangaroo. I have been sent here by a dermaiden, half human and half dolphin, named Rosaline to save you.

Rosaline has sensed the message from a marble man named Simon that you were in danger.

"How did he do it that fast?"

Their signals can travel as fast as the speed of sound during danger. When Simon got knocked out, his signal traveled to Rosaline and then to me. I have the ability to appear and disappear at will.

"I see."

Climb onto my back. I am going to take you to Dermand Island, about ten kilometers away from Yanowic. Dermaidens don't like to travel to islands or lands populated by humans, so I have to take you to where Rosaline can meet you.

"What's Rosaline going to do?"

She's going to break the sleeping spell that the dingo has given Simon and the couple. When the dingo stabs or bites someone, that person falls asleep and can't wake up for twenty-four hours. Only this magic seaweed called adormos seaweed, found near the reefs of Dermand, can break that spell.

Regulus leaned his head down, and his beak touched the ground.

Alyssa's stomach compressed. While she didn't fear heights on thrill rides at amusement parks, she disliked experiencing elevation without any safety precautions. She'd never even been able to jump off high dives at swimming pools because of how the boards had stood several feet above the ground, and she'd been on her own. Nevertheless, she climbed onto Regulus's back and slid behind his neck. "Don't fly too high."

Regulus nodded. He picked up his front feet and dug them into the sand. Alyssa hugged his neck and bumped against his back as he sped up his legs. Regulus galloped into the water and splashed onto Alyssa's legs. His pace increased the rapidity of Alyssa's posting up and down on his back. He flapped his wings, fanning Alyssa on the cheeks. His back legs pressed into the underwater sand. He lifted his front legs off the ground, and Alyssa inhaled. Then he tilted as his back legs kicked out the water.

Regulus continued to flap as he flew farther away from the ground. Alyssa screamed as Regulus ascended until they were about a hundred feet above the water. But her noise didn't seem to bother him. She yelped until her mouth dried out, and she coughed.

Just keep holding on, and you'll be fine, she told herself.

Alyssa grabbed Regulus's neck and breathed. Her muscles loosened. She smiled, thinking about Regulus like a roller coaster but without the hills or loops.

Minutes had passed, and Alyssa noticed an island. It looked like Yanowic with the palm trees on the large beach and the forest behind it. But there were no humans or any signs of civilization, and the island appeared smaller than Yanowic.

Regulus tilted his head forward. He glided toward the ocean and lowered. Alyssa thought of him like an airplane based on how he landed and slowed down. Regulus flapped as he approached the water near the shore. Alyssa stared down and noticed that the ground seemed close enough that she could jump off him and land safely—not that she would, though.

Regulus landed on his front legs onto the sand, followed by his hind legs. He trotted, and Alyssa bumped against him again. He steadied down and stopped. Then he lowered his head onto the sand. Alyssa figured out that he likely wanted her to slide off him. So she did and then noticed words forming on his leg band.

I am going to close my eyes for about a minute. Please do not disturb me since I will be sending a signal to Rosaline to let her know that you're here on Dermand Island.

Alyssa looked up and nodded. She sat on the sand and watched Regulus shut his eyes. Would Rosaline comprehend Alyssa, though? If dermaidens didn't like going to places with civilizations, then how would they understand English? Did they speak their own language—or not talk at all?

A woman sang the tune of "Wishing You Were Somehow Here Again" from *The Phantom of the Opera*, and Alyssa looked up. It seemed to come from the ocean, although Rosaline or any other dermaiden couldn't possibly sing a showtune. No exposure to developed civilizations must mean no knowledge of any song humans had created—unless dermaidens had the ability to magically absorb them. Anything could happen with enchanted creatures' skills.

The song grew louder. Alyssa stood up, focusing on the voice. There was still no hint of who sang it. But what human would ever sing and not reveal him or herself while swimming to a deserted island? According to what Isabelle had said yesterday, no wizard could exceed in basic skills, like swimming, more than any ordinary person. That meant the song had to come from a dermaiden. Dermaidens somehow seemed to know how to capture songs from plays and memorize them.

A dolphin fluke lifted itself from the water as the song loudened, but the sound faded. Alyssa didn't know what Rosaline looked like, so that could either be her or another dermaiden. Alyssa turned to Regulus, whose eyes were now open, and his head turned to the water. If Rosaline hadn't arrived, then Regulus would still do what he'd done before the voice sang.

The fluke sunk, and the song stopped. A woman poked her head out of the water. She swam closer, and Alyssa observed her. Her platinum-blonde hair flowed about a few inches past the top of her tail. Bubblegum-pink patches covered her cheeks, the edges blending in with her skin. Deep red lips contrasted with her hair and cheeks. Light-blue lemon-shaped spots surrounded her eyes. Her eyelashes looked thick as if she had applied too much mascara. She also wore a strapless bikini top. Alyssa assumed that all those colors on her face didn't result from make-up since that would wash out in the water.

The dermaiden spoke a strange language in a high soft-spoken voice. Alyssa tilted her head and widened her mouth. The dermaiden sighed and moved her hands around, creating a glass cube filled with bright purple smoke. Then she lifted it up, looking into Alyssa's eyes.

"You want me to take it?" Alyssa asked.

The lady nodded. Alyssa guessed that she understood English, even if she might not speak it. Alyssa took the cube and watched words spell out on it:

My name is Rosaline, and I'm a dermaiden, half human and half dolphin, as Regulus's band must have told you. I am known for singing, saving people, and taming magical creatures.

I speak Dermese, the dermaiden language, but can understand most languages in the Indo- Pacific. I hope Regulus sent out the message I told him to send you.

Alyssa looked up at Rosaline. "He did." She paused. "How'd you know that *Phantom of the Opera* song?"

Rosaline spoke her language for about twenty seconds, which caused words to appear in the cube.

Dermaidens have special powers to hear and absorb music and intelligence from humans on the land and remember them. They sing songs they know to attract attention from the ones they're looking for or rescuing. I heard that song a few years ago at a theater in Australia and liked it so much, it was absorbed into my brain, and now I like to sing it.

"Cool. So can you get the seaweed to wake my mentors up, please?"

Rosaline spoke. Her translation spelled out into the cube.

I can, but I need help from my sister, Penelope. I forgot that my father had decreased my magic skills because I had lied to him a week ago about something. I'll go get Penelope.

Rosaline turned around and dunked her head into the water. As she swam away, she sang the tune of "I Dreamed a Dream" from *Les Misérables*.

About five minutes later, Rosaline returned with Penelope. Penelope's bangs and shoulder-length black hair formed an arch around her head, which contrasted with her hot-pink lips, coral-colored cheek spots, and green patches surrounding her eyes. Penelope also wore a belly T-shirt. She spoke to Rosaline about something, and out of her mouth came a low voice. Wow! Had Alyssa only seen them at first sight, she would never have thought that they were sisters.

Rosaline received the seaweed from Penelope and spoke to Alyssa as she looked into the cube.

Penelope and I are going to knot the seaweed and then tie them together. Then, after we think of the spell, a glitter lamb will form. Glitter lambs have always succeeded at breaking the sleeping spell. The lamb will travel all the way to Yanowic to wake up the marble figure and anyone else sleeping. But first you'll need to tell us their names, what they look like, and what they're wearing.

Alyssa told Rosaline everything she'd requested. Penelope then smiled and said something, which Alyssa guessed was "Thank you."

Then Penelope and Rosaline made five knots in the seaweed and tied them together so that they attached. They pulled the plant and shut their eyes. They hummed a random tune, which they softened but loudened every second. Gold glitter rose out of the palms of their hands and circled as they ascended. The specks formed a spiral and widened, creating the shape of a hurricane.

Alyssa opened her mouth as Penelope and Rosaline lowered their hands, making the glitter rain out of its shape. But it stopped in the air, sticking together and forming another shape. A snout, sheep-like ears, short tail, and cloven hooves revealed to Alyssa that the glitter produced the lamb. The creation opened its mouth and let out a *baa*.

"Wow," whispered Alyssa.

Penelope spoke to the lamb in Dermese, and it galloped into the air, releasing specks along its path. It ran farther away, and Penelope and Rosaline turned back to Alyssa and said something to her. Alyssa looked into the cube, staring at the sentences produced.

When the lamb arrives at Yanowic, it'll explode into glitter. That glitter will break the sleeping spell cast on those under it and wake them up.

Alyssa nodded and looked into the cube. Penelope's words faded, and Rosaline's words replaced them.

Regulus can now take you back to Yanowic. I'm afraid I must go since I promised Penelope that I'd do something with her.

Alyssa looked up at Rosaline. "That's fine. Thanks, guys."
Rosaline and Penelope waved and turned back to the ocean. They dove underwater and swam away. Alyssa turned to Regulus, who lowered his head. She climbed onto him, and he prepared to take off back to Yanowic.

11

Now back on Yanowic, Alyssa slid off Regulus's back and turned to the glitter lamb. She smiled as she watched it gallop toward her mentors. But something hard hit her on the back, and she jerked forward. She turned around. Regulus's leg band formed words.

I am going to go now. Goodbye and good luck.

"Bye," said Alyssa. "Thank you."

Regulus flapped and lifted himself up into the air.

Alyssa gazed at him until the lamb made its high *baa* sound again. It exploded into specks, which sprinkled onto Mathias, Simon, and Isabelle. Not only that—the wounds they'd received from the dingo shrank and vanished. All three yawned and stretched. They lifted themselves up and turned to Alyssa.

"Blimey, Alyssa, you're all right," said Simon.

"What have you been doing this whole time?" Mathias asked.

"You really want to know?" Alyssa asked.

"Yes, of course," said Mathias.

Alyssa told them everything from the time Regulus had killed the dingo to when he had brought her back here. Isabelle and Mathias looked at Simon.

"How'd you know that dermaiden?" asked Isabelle.

"I didn't," said Simon. "Sending out messages to strangers during danger is just an instinct in marble figures."

"Well, we all ought to thank Simon for this," said Mathias.

Everyone thanked him and walked back to where Isabelle had dropped her stuff. Nothing had been damaged, so she picked up the supplies and led Alyssa into her tube.

"I'll meet you at the dark magic center, Mathias," said Isabelle as Mathias hopped into his tube.

Now outside the dark magic center, Isabelle and Mathias led Alyssa and Simon to a tree.

"I'm going to give you guys invisibility ponchos and make you air screens to watch us," said Isabelle.

"Isabelle, I was thinking that they should watch us from inside," said Mathias.

"Mathias, it's too dangerous, especially for Alyssa," said Isabelle.

"But she and Simon would be wearing the ponchos," Mathias said.

"This is much safer, though." Isabelle pointed her wand at Alyssa and let an air bubble out, which expanded to the size of Simon's tablet. Then she did the same thing to Simon and then gave him and Alyssa ponchos. "Put these on and don't make any sounds."

Alyssa and Simon nodded.

"But then how do we hear what you're doing?" Alyssa asked.

"I'm creating wireless earbuds," Isabelle directed her wand into her palm. She made the buds and handed a pair each to Simon and Alyssa. "You'll also be able to see both of us after we separate."

"How?" asked Alyssa.

"The screen will divide," said Isabelle.

Alyssa nodded.

"Good luck," whispered Simon.

Isabelle and Mathias disappeared. Alyssa pulled her poncho on and gasped since her body could no longer be seen. But she put on the hood and zipped it to hide her face. She sat back down and put in her earbuds. She saw only Isabelle on her screen, wearing her poncho and leaning against the main hallway wall. Mathias probably did the same thing.

"David, how could you forget about the dingo I hooked up to the computer?" asked a woman with a Southern American accent.

"Relax, Clarissa," said David as he and Clarissa walked down the main hallway.

"You didn't even find another creature," she said.

"I did, but it ran away too fast."

Isabelle stuck her wand out and whipped it around. The same orange sand that had knocked out Hailey and Uncle Bruce swirled and knocked out Clarissa. Mathias repeated the same to David. Isabelle knelt by Clarissa and stuck her hand out to rub the skin with a rubbing stick. The stick turned the orange tip dark blue. She and Mathias rubbed the couple's skin and then kicked the two, took off their ponchos, and covered them.

Alyssa's heart palpitated as Isabelle and Mathias stood in the middle of the hallway—visible. What if someone caught them?

Especially—Master Beau? They seemed fine now, but that could change any moment.

Isabelle pulled out two tiny paper cups and poured some of the Impersonaide potion in hers and Mathias's. Then the two stuck their sticks inside, lightening the liquid to a light caramel brown. They held the stick in for about three seconds and then drank the potion.

Air swept up from their feet to their heads like wind blowing from the ground. Mathias's skin had paled, and his hair was gone. Isabelle had curly chestnut hair midway down her back. She also had freckles and a few pimples. They also wore the same clothes David and Clarissa wore.

"Shall we go find someone?" asked Mathias in the same voice and accent as David.

"Yes," said Isabelle, who had the same voice and accent as Clarissa.

She and Mathias walked down the hallway but stopped at the end where one could only walk left or right.

"Where should we go?" asked Mathias.

"I don't know," said Isabelle.

"David, Clarissa, what are you two doing?" asked a strange man with a British accent.

"Seamus, don't you have any work to do?" Master Beau popped his head out of his office door.

"Right, I forgot to practice the wart-making spell on those lobsters," said Seamus.

"Go do that," said Master Beau.

Seamus walked down the left hallway.

"David, Clarissa, what can I do to help you?" asked Master Beau.

"Where's your computer?" Mathias asked.

"You didn't look up anything else on making magical connections to children?" asked Master Beau.

"I'll do it now," said Mathias.

"Go downstairs and do it," said Master Beau.

"Okay," said Mathias.

"Clarissa, I'm going to be taking a quick coffee break," said Master Beau. "In the meantime, can you finish the ingredients to my potion?"

"What potion?" asked Isabelle.

"Oh, I never told you," said Master Beau. "It's called Expugnato potion. When Alyssa and the other four children I select drink this potion, they will be loyal to me and will accept everything I do to them, including harm."

Alyssa gasped.

"They'll be willing to sacrifice themselves to anything I send to destroy them, and then . . . my dream of being France's dictator will come true."

"Oh my god," said Isabelle.

"I know. Isn't it exciting?"

"Can I wait for you inside your potion room?" asked Isabelle.

"Sure." Master Beau walked back into his office.

Alyssa's screen divided into two; one side revealed Mathias walking in the basement, and the other showed Isabelle opening the potion room.

Isabelle strode inside, looking around at the shelves of various potions in plastic bottles and the labeled boxes of potion ingredients. Near the corner stood a large silver pot with lit buttons along the side and tubes on both ends leading up to a microwave and a blender. Isabelle strode toward it and leaned down at it. It was labeled "Brewbot 3000" and inside was a plum-colored liquid, as thick as spaghetti sauce. Isabelle whipped her wand around, which let out pink smoke. The potion evaporated into purple steam as the smoke clouded above it.

Alyssa turned to the screen with Mathias. *He walked into the room with the brain-domination computer. The wires attached to it were limp on the floor. Mathias pointed his wand at it, sweat pouring down his cheeks.*

But Master Beau threw the door open and glowered at Mathias. "David, what are you doing?"

Mathias turned to him. "I was trying to save—" *He covered his mouth, and Master Beau strode over to him, still glaring.*

"Who would you be trying to save?" he asked.

"No one," Mathias rushed the words out of his mouth.

Master Beau took out his cell phone and texted someone. "Seamus is coming with Veriforce potion."

"Why?"

"I suspect you're not really David."

"Yes, of course I am."

Seamus appeared. "Hello, Master Beau." *He handed him a bottle of fizzy golden-yellow liquid.*

Mathias held out his wand. "I don't need it!"

"Amittere obiectum!" Master Beau zapped Mathias's wand out of his hand.

Seamus grabbed him and held his back against his chest.

"Let go of me!" yelled Mathias.

Master Beau opened the bottle and squeezed Mathias's nose. Mathias opened his mouth as Master Beau poured the potion down his throat.

"Are you really David Willis?" Master Beau asked.

"No," Mathias answered.

"Who are you?"

"Mathias Williams."

"And who are you trying to save?"

"Alyssa McCarthy."

"I knew you weren't David!" snarled Master Beau.

Mathias picked up his wand and ran out.

Alyssa turned to see the screen with Isabelle.

The potion was gone. Nothing remained in the pot. But Master Beau appeared with the Veriforce potion and gasped. "Clarissa, what are you doing?"

"Nothing."

"Wait—are you really Clarissa Murphy?"

"Yeah, of course," said Isabelle.

"We'll see about that." Master Beau grabbed Isabelle and held her against him. He squeezed her nose and poured the potion down her throat.

"What is your name?"

"Isabelle Cunningham."

"Are you trying to save Alyssa McCarthy?"

"Yes."

"I knew it!"

Isabelle held out her arms and disappeared outside, where Mathias leaned against a tree.

"Let's drink the Normalla potion and get out of here," said Isabelle.

The two poured the potion and drank it. Air swept from their feet to their heads and returned them to their true identities.

The screens disappeared, and Alyssa looked up, watching Isabelle and Mathias race each other toward her and Simon.

"Take your ponchos off," said Isabelle.

Alyssa unzipped hers and peeled it off. Simon did the same thing.

"We need to get out of here before anything happens," said Isabelle.

Simon followed Mathias into his tube, and Alyssa followed Isabelle into hers.

"I can't believe what Master Beau did." Alyssa put her seatbelt on.   "Mathias didn't even destroy the computer."

"We'll have to come back tonight." Isabelle pressed the take-off button, making the tube lift into the air.

*   *   *   *

An hour had passed since everyone had left the dark magic center. They had consumed just sandwiches and veggie sticks at lunchtime. Now that everybody had cleaned up, he or she headed into the living room. Simon had finished eating earlier than the others, so he sat on a couch and listened to his WiPod.

"Simon?" Alyssa asked.

He took out his earbuds and turned to her. "Yes?"

"Can we see what Master Beau's doing?"

"Oh, sure." Simon picked up his tablet and flew out of the bedroom. Alyssa, Mathias, and Isabelle gathered around him as he turned on the device and opened his tracking app, where he selected the Video option.

Master Beau stood outside with David, Clarissa, and Seamus. "Do you two want to thank Seamus for waking you guys up with the Weckis weed?" he asked David and Clarissa.

They thanked Seamus.

"Seamus also bought an illegal app where you can search someone's name, age, and address, and find out what they've been doing for up to the past week," said Master Beau. "He found out online that if you want to rule an entire nation, every person you select must have interacted with your target within the past week. Otherwise, the connections won't be strong enough and your power won't work well. Now I already plan to kidnap Alyssa's cousin, but now Seamus is going to read the names of the other kids, and then I'll assign to each of who you'll kidnap."

Alyssa gulped.

"Okay, guys, the names of the other children are Jasmine Wilson, Destiny Cox, and Madison Jennings."

83

"No," squeaked Alyssa.

Then Master Beau assigned who'd abduct whom. David would take Jasmine, Clarissa would kidnap Destiny, and Seamus would get Madison.

"Did you remember to make the connections?" asked Clarissa.

"Uh huh," said Master Beau. "I did it last night."

"Well, at least we have those charms around us," said Seamus. "So we can't get arrested."

"Aren't there charms around your helicopter too?" asked Clarissa.

"Yes," said Master Beau. "But the good news is that I've figured out how to make portals on land. I was practicing a lot last night."

"We don't know how to make them though," said David.

"How about I show you all before I kidnap Alyssa's cousin?" asked Master Beau. "We'll hide somewhere and practice."

"Where?" asked Clarissa.

"The middle of a national park would do," said Master Beau. "But it'll take several hours."

"Good thing we can't get jetlagged," said Clarissa. "Half the other wizards in the world aren't lucky about that."

"So let's disappear to New Jersey," said Master Beau.

All four vanished.

"What the heck?" shrieked Alyssa. "They can't do that!"

"They've already disappeared." Simon closed his app.

"Can't we stop them?" asked Alyssa.

"It's illegal for wizards to disappear into other countries," said Isabelle. "They have charms to protect themselves, but we can't perform those charms on ourselves."

"It's very hard to do, and no one would ever teach anyone those charms," said Mathias.

"So . . . we're going to have to let them . . . hurt my cousin and everyone else?" Alyssa asked, her voice breaking.

"No," said Isabelle. "When they come back, we'll protect those girls."

"Can't you call your pilot?" asked Alyssa.

"We can't leave you behind," said Isabelle. "And even if we could leave the country, Master Beau and his workers can't be seen by the police or government."

Tears spilled from Alyssa's eyes. "There's got to be a way."

"There isn't." Mathias shook his head. "We're so sorry."

Alyssa burst into tears. She ran into the bedroom and threw herself onto her bed. Tears soaked her arm as she covered her eyes with it.

Why did this have to happen? How was there nothing she could do? She wished that she could just find some way to overthrow Master Beau. She desired to have enough strength to break the wall. She wanted all this to stop. But it didn't seem like this would end soon.

12

Fifteen minutes had passed since Alyssa had cried. Isabelle had offered her chamomile tea. She poured sugar out of her wand into a mug as Alyssa sat at the table. Then she created the teabag, boiling water, and a lemon and stirred them with a spoon.

"I really wish there were a way to stop Master Beau from kidnapping your cousin and friends," said Isabelle.

"The government won't make exceptions for emergencies?"

"The prime minister of Yanowic is very protected. No one's allowed to see him unless they work for him."

"Why?"

"In the past, Yanowic's prime ministers have been lured into a lot of trouble by the citizens. So about fifteen years ago, a new law passed to only allow people who work for the prime ministers to see them."

"Oh."

"But once we find out that Master Beau and his workers have brought them to the dark magic center, we'll take them and protect them here."

"Are we going to be able to defeat Master Beau?"

"Well, I don't like the idea of hurting him directly. But we'll brainstorm some indirect ways to defeat him."

Alyssa nodded and sipped her tea. She drank it for about twenty minutes and then headed into the bedroom.

Simon lay on his bed, listening to his WiPod. He turned to Alyssa, still wearing his earbuds. "Hello."

"Hey." Alyssa sat on her bed.

"Are you feeling better?"

"Sort of."

"I have some ideas to keep you occupied and feel better at the same time. We could watch something funny on the Enchanted World Network. That's the general term for our Internet. The Magic Carpet World Connections is just one of the browsers."

"I don't want to watch anything." Alyssa shook her head.

"How about some music? I have a playlist of relaxing music on my WiPod. Or do you prefer pop when you're upset?"

"Simon, you've got to understand that when someone is worried about their loved ones, distracting them isn't necessarily the right thing."

"Really? Well, it's always worked for marble figures."

"I'm not a marble figure, though."

"Alyssa, don't tell me that I'm no help at all." Simon arched his eyebrows.

"It's not that. I just—"

"So you're just trying to be polite by saying I am a help when I'm really not?"

"Simon, relax."

"Don't talk balderdash with me." Simon crossed his arms. "You'd probably rather sit and worry about those girls than find a way to cheer yourself up."

"Those girls are important to me."

"So you're saying I'm not important to you at all? I'm just a piece of rubbish?"

"No, of course not. Simon, I think you're overreacting."

"You're the one being underappreciative!" Simon raised his voice.

"All right, sorry. I . . . I didn't mean it."

"Well, whether you meant it or not, you still did it. You do whatever you want. I'm leaving this room."

"Fine." Alyssa bent her eyebrows.

Simon flew out.

Alyssa lay on her bed and breathed. Who was to blame? Simon or herself? She considered herself right that distractions didn't always work when somebody was worried. Yet, she chose to wait at least a few minutes before she could show herself to Simon since he probably wouldn't want to talk now.

"Simon, are you okay?" Mathias asked.

"Leave me alone," he said.

"Why are you in a bad mood?" asked Isabelle.

"Alyssa's underappreciative," Simon said. "I offered her ways to feel better and—"

"Simon, sometimes that doesn't work," said Isabelle. "There are times people just need to find their own ways to calm down."

"That's what Alyssa said," Simon said.

"And I think she's right," said Mathias.

Alyssa poked her head out of the bedroom.

Simon looked at her. "I'm sorry, Alyssa. I was being a jerk."

"That's okay," she said. "Hey, can you make an alarm on your tablet to go off when Master Beau and his workers come back?"

"I don't think so," said Simon. "But I'll take a look at what he and his workers are doing every hour."

"Good," said Alyssa. "Thank you."

*   *   *   *

Until everybody had fallen asleep, Simon had checked on Master Beau and his staff every hour. He'd still stood in an open field surrounded by woodlands and practiced making portals. But he might do something else now.

Alyssa tossed and turned in her bed. She had no idea what time it was, and without windows, she couldn't figure it out. It might be seven a.m., or it could be two a.m. She stretched and lifted her body. Glancing at the clock in front of her, she saw that it was six-thirty. She turned to Simon, Mathias, and Isabelle, who still slept. Sweat patched her face, and even the inside of her T-shirt and sweat shorts.

She turned to Simon's tablet on the nightstand next to her since Simon slept on the middle bed. Simon didn't move or make any sounds anyway. But Alyssa would only check to see what Master Beau did. He may still work on the portals. He might take Hailey while his workers kidnapped the other girls. He could have even returned.

Alyssa reached her trembling hands out and grabbed the tablet. She pulled it toward her and hopped out of bed, holding the object. Turning back, she saw Simon toss, and her chest stung. But she continued to tiptoe out of the bedroom and shut the door.

She stared at the screen. While she'd borrowed friends' cell phones and sometimes even iPods in the past, she'd never used an electronic tablet. Did a guide directing how to use the Triton's Tablet come with it? Simon hadn't carried one when he'd first brought it.

She pressed the bottom button in the middle, which caused the tablet to turn on. A red screen came on with an arrow pointing right. It said, "Slide to unlock." Alyssa did that and saw a spy person icon with a large hat and a long coat on the screensaver. Underneath, it said, "Tracking App." Alyssa pressed that and received a map of where Master Beau was. And guess where he'd gone . . .

"He got Hailey," gasped Alyssa.

According to the beige screen, Master Beau led Hailey into the backyard. Uh oh. He hadn't put her under a spell, right?

Blood rushing through her veins, Alyssa ran back into the bedroom and swung the door open. She slammed it shut, and everyone else woke up.

"Alyssa, what are you doing?" Mathias lifted himself up.

"We've got to go to the dark magic center now," said Alyssa.

"Did you look at my tablet?" asked Simon.

"Yeah," said Alyssa. "You were sleeping, so I didn't want to wake you up."

"You still should've asked me," said Simon.

"I'm sorry, but Simon's right," said Mathias.

"Sorry," said Alyssa.

"Alyssa, why don't Mathias and I go while you and Simon stay behind?" Isabelle sat up.

"Why do you want them to stay behind?" asked Mathias.

"Because I don't want—"

"Why can't they just stay under invisibility ponchos?" asked Mathias. "Isabelle, you have so many."

Isabelle sighed. "All right, we'll all go. Let's get ready."

Alyssa did her morning routine and put on a tank top and short leggings. Everybody else got ready as well for the next five minutes or so. Isabelle created granola bars for everybody to munch on during the ride. Looking at hers, though, Alyssa felt her throat burn. Her stomach often couldn't handle food if she'd woken up at this time.

Alyssa stepped outside with the others and watched Isabelle shrink the tent. Then she followed her to her tube while Mathias took Simon. She hopped into the back and buckled up. Isabelle jumped into the pilot's seat, put the ponchos next to her, and pressed the button to take off.

Thoughts of what Master Beau and his workers would do to Hailey, Destiny, Jasmine, and Madison, raced inside Alyssa's head. Where would he keep them? Would Isabelle and Mathias be able to save them? What if Master Beau hid them and wouldn't tell her and her mentors where they were until they died? When Alyssa had lost her parents and aunt, she'd experienced depression and sometimes even shock. Ever since those times, she had hoped to never lose a loved one again.

Minutes had passed, and Isabelle landed outside the dark magic center. She turned off the tube and hopped out, carrying the ponchos. Mathias had arrived before her and stood with Simon outside his tube.

"Hey, Isabelle, I was thinking about having Alyssa come with us instead," he said.

"Mathias, are you crazy?" asked Isabelle. "She'll be caught and taken from us."

"Well, I don't think her friends will trust us unless they see her," said Mathias. "They need to know that we're not going to hurt them. So I want Alyssa to come."

"What if we tell them we know her?" asked Isabelle.

"I don't think that's enough," said Mathias. "I think the other girls will be more comfortable if they see her."

"All right, Mathias," Isabelle frowned. "But then Alyssa must stay inside her poncho until we find the girls."

"But that'll startle them," said Mathias.

"They already know about magic," said Isabelle. "I don't have time for this discussion. We've got to go." She threw Alyssa and Simon ponchos. "Put these on."

They did so and headed inside the building. Blood zoomed through Alyssa's veins. Her heartbeat spread from her chest to her throat. So far, no one roamed or stood in the main hallway.

But a beep went off, and Alyssa turned to where it came from. A camera leaned down from the wall and flashed its tiny red light. Someone appeared out of the air, and that was Master Beau. The beeping ended.

"What are you all doing here?" asked Master Beau. "I know there are four of you. These cameras my workers have installed last night can see under invisibility ponchos."

"You let those girls go," Mathias took down his poncho hood.

"No!" yelled Master Beau. "Wait a minute—how do you know about the girls? Are you that guy who stole one of the workers' identity?"

"Why would I answer that?" asked Mathias.

"That tells me you are, and now you want to save them. Well, forget it." He held out his wand.

"*Amittere obiectum!*" Isabelle whipped her wand and zapped Master Beau's out of his hand. But he picked it up.

"*Somnum harena!*" Master Beau pointed his wand at Isabelle.

Sand swirled out, and as it neared Isabelle's eyes, Mathias cried, *"Duratus nunco!"* which froze the sand in the air. Isabelle backed away.

Mathias then whipped his wand around, but nothing happened.

"Are you trying to put me under a spell?" asked Master Beau.

"Yes," replied Mathias.

"I've already been under a spell," said Master Beau. "Now all of you get out."

Alyssa heard Simon mumble something, and she and the others turned to his sound. But everyone turned back to Master Beau. A mug of hot tea floated over his head.

"What are you all looking at?" Master Beau asked.

A crack formed on the mug and spread throughout it. A piece chipped off, and the clay shattered. Tea poured onto Master Beau's head. He screamed and covered his face.

Isabelle and Mathias ran away from him. Alyssa followed them.

"Where's he keeping them?" Mathias stopped at the end of the main hallway.

"You idiots!" screamed Master Beau. "Get out of here!"

"Somnum harena!" Mathias whipped his wand around.

The sand swirled, and Master Beau fell asleep.

"We should be safe now," said Mathias.

"What are two doing here?" David stood outside of a door down the hallway across from them.

Mathias whipped his wand and turned David's pupils blue.

"Are you looking for the girls we captured?" asked David.

"Yes," said Mathias.

"They're in the prison room upstairs, behind the third door on your left," said David.

"Thank you." Mathias led everyone upstairs. "Alyssa and Simon, take off your ponchos."

They removed them.

"By the way, guys—that was me who created that cup of tea over Master Beau's head," said Simon.

"Thanks for telling us," said Isabelle. "But we need to hurry up and get these girls out."

"Wait—you don't have the other ponchos," said Alyssa.

"That's okay," said Isabelle. "I can make them appear here."

Mathias turned the doorknob and grunted. "It's locked." He let go.

Isabelle pointed her wand at it. "*Patefacio sursum.*"

The doorknob snapped, and she opened the door. Stepping inside, Alyssa saw Destiny, Madison, Jasmine, and Hailey behind the bars and chained to the wall.

"Oh my God, Alyssa, you're here!" cried Madison.

"We're going to get you girls out of here." Isabelle pointed her wand at the cover over the button. "*Patefacio sursum.*" The handle to the padlock lifted, and she took it off.

Alyssa looked around. "Where's Simon?"

"I put my poncho back on," he whispered. "I don't want to scare the girls now."

Alyssa turned back to the bars. They rose above the ground.

"Mathias, break their chains," said Isabelle.

He nodded and pointed his wand at them. He whipped it around, and their chains dissolved into dust. They bolted up and ran outside.

Hailey threw her arms around Alyssa. "I missed you."

"Me too," said Alyssa.

The two broke up their hug.

"All right, guys, we need to get out of here before anything happens," said Isabelle. "I was going to give you all invisibility ponchos, but I don't have time right now." She opened the door and led everybody out.

They hurried down the stairs and through the main hallway, where Master Beau still slept. The light on the camera flashed and beeped as they passed it.   But they ran back to the tubes, and no threats approached them. However, Alyssa still thought about what might occur later.

13

The other girls had reacted the same way as Alyssa to all the rooms under the tent. They drank the Chronocurrent potion. Then they entered the kitchen for breakfast.

Simon ate bacon and eggs. The girls jumped and screamed.

"I'm sorry if I scared you all," said Simon.

"Is that a talking statue?" yelped Destiny.

"No, I'm a marble figure," said Simon. "I don't like being called a statue. Anyway, do you remember Alyssa leaning down before we left?"

"Yes," said Destiny.

"I'd told her not to mention me to you guys until we came back," Simon said.

"That was stupid," said Destiny.

"Whatever," said Simon.

Isabelle created the girls what they wanted for breakfast, and then they all introduced themselves to her, Simon, and Mathias. Isabelle then told them not to tell anyone at home about magical technology or creations.

"What time is it in New Jersey?" asked Mathias.

"It was afternoon when Master Beau kidnapped me," said Hailey.

"Oh—how's your dad?" asked Madison.

"We're considering an assisted living home from him in Opal Stream," said Hailey. "He can't really learn too much anymore."

"That's horrible," said Jasmine.

"Is Opal Stream where you're living now?" Madison asked.

"I'm staying there while my grandparents apply to be my legal guardians," said Hailey. She turned to Alyssa. "Alyssa, I found that letter from your godfather on the kitchen counter."

"Okay," she said.

"I called him and told him to call my grandparents' number from now on," said Hailey.

"You didn't tell him where I was, did you?"

"No—I just told him you were busy. He didn't ask for anything else."

"That's strange." Alyssa drank her pineapple juice.

"So what's the deal with sleeping assignments?" asked Madison.

"Wait—we don't have anything with us," said Jasmine.

"I can get your things after breakfast if you give me your addresses," said Simon.

"Can you take us back?" asked Jasmine.

"I'm afraid I can't, sorry," Simon frowned. "One, I'm too small. Two, because you're not sorceresses, you can't magically disappear."

"Wait, Simon—isn't it illegal to disappear into another country?" asked Alyssa.

"Marble figures can get away with loads of things, Alyssa. I'll bring an invisibility poncho to hide from other people. When no one else is around, though, I will pack what the girls need and then disappear with their bags."

"How are you going to help us all at once?" asked Madison.

"I'm not," said Simon. "I'm going to do one at a time."

After breakfast, Simon asked the girls who wanted to receive their stuff first. They all wanted to, but Simon chose to start with Hailey. She told him the house address and listed what she needed. He grabbed a poncho and disappeared.

"Okay, girls, while Simon's gone, why don't we give you all your sleeping places?" asked Isabelle. "Alyssa, you can share your bed with Hailey."

Alyssa nodded.

"Madison and Jasmine, you two share the middle bed," said Isabelle.

"Isn't that where Simon is sleeping, though?" asked Alyssa.

"I'm sure he won't mind sleeping somewhere else," said Mathias.

"Where's he going to sleep?" asked Alyssa.

"Either Mathias or I will buy him a sleeping bag." Isabelle turned to Destiny. "Destiny, you'll be sleeping on the couch."

"What?" asked Destiny. "Why can't you create me a big bed with a canopy, like what I have at home?"

"Because wizards can't create expensive objects they don't already own," said Isabelle.

"Can't Alyssa and Hailey give up their bed?"

"Destiny, deal with what I gave you for now," said Isabelle. "Alyssa and Hailey are not giving up their bed for you."

94

"But I hate sleeping on couches," Destiny said.

"It rolls out into a bed," said Isabelle.

"Come on, Destiny, it's great when you get to be by yourself," said Madison.

"Yeah, but not when you have something you don't like," said Destiny.

"It's only for now," Isabelle said. "You'll get to sleep in the bed you like when you go home."

"Speaking of home—do you think that invisible wall will keep them from leaving this country too?" Alyssa referred to the other girls.

"Good point," said Isabelle. "We'll have to check."

"How are we going to do that?" asked Jasmine.

"Maybe Simon will find out for us." Alyssa then told them about his tablet.

"Well, I hope the wall goes down soon," said Jasmine. "I don't like being in a fantasy-like environment. It's one thing to read books or watch movies about them, but being surrounded by magic in real life—that's just weird and pretty scary."

"I liked that Isabelle was able to create our breakfast just with her wand," said Madison.

"Hello, everyone." Simon stood there with Hailey's suitcase and old backpack from school.

"Thanks," said Hailey.

"No problem," said Simon.

Over the next half hour, Simon left to get Madison, Jasmine, and Destiny's stuff. The girls unpacked and changed into summer clothes for about twenty minutes until Simon decided to take out his tablet to show them what Master Beau was doing. He explained to the girls how the tracking app worked.

Master Beau stood in what looked like a conference room with all his workers seated in chairs. His arms were crossed, and he wore a glare on his face.

Alyssa figured that someone had used the Wekis weed to wake him up.

"Who told Alyssa McCarthy's mentors where the girls were?" growled Master Beau.

"Mathias Williams put me under a spell," said David. "I would never have told him on my own."

"Why didn't you stop him, David?" snapped Master Beau.

"I . . . I didn't know he'd do it."

"I'm putting you on probation," said Master Beau. "You have one month to do everything right. Otherwise, you're fired."

"I found a creature and tranquilized it," said Clarissa.

"What kind of creature is it?" asked Master Beau.

"A Cyclops frog," responded Clarissa. "I was thinking that maybe you should hurt Alyssa's mentors first before you hurt her and her friends."

"But they're always with the girls," Master Beau said.

"Cyclops frogs have the power to hypnotize people into coming to them," said Seamus.

"Wow, I didn't know that," said Master Beau.

"Why don't you also make the frog hypnotize the girls into ignoring their mentors while they get attacked?" asked Clarissa.

"Good plan," said Master Beau. "Is the frog hooked up to the computer?"

"Yes," said Clarissa.

"Perfect," said Master Beau. "This meeting is over. You can all take your coffee break while I work on the computer."

Everyone gasped.

"What are we going to do?" asked Hailey as Simon closed the app.

"We're going to have to make a potion to create a shield," said Isabelle.

"Do you have a Brewbot?" asked Mathias.

"I can go buy one while you stay behind," said Isabelle. "I haven't been to Arietta's in a year."

"What's that?" asked Hailey.

"It's a huge magical department store," said Isabelle. "It's kind of like Costco with all the different things you can buy. You have to be a member to go there."

"It's also invisible to ordinary people." Mathias turned to Isabelle. "Do you want to renew your membership?"

"I can do that online." Isabelle sat down and made her laptop appear on her lap.

"Isabelle, what if the frog comes before you make the potion?" asked Alyssa. "We need to have a backup plan."

"I can let you know when the frog is released from Master Beau's computer," said Simon. "Then we'll all hide in the bedroom under invisibility ponchos."

"What if the frog sees through it?" asked Hailey.

"They can't see through closed doors," said Simon. "I'll assure you that."

"How do you know?" Hailey asked.

"I had to read about them for a magic science project in marble figure university," said Simon.

"Those exist?" asked Destiny.

"Yes." Simon frowned. "They're in wilderness areas and protected by a shield so that humans can't see them."

"That sounds tough," said Madison.

"It was," Simon said. "If we wanted to leave school grounds, the attendance office had to approve of where we were going. They could only be places in the wizarding world."

"Wow," said Madison.

"Okay, everyone, I renewed my account at Arietta's," Isabelle said. "I'm going to go. If I'm not back before the frog, you should all hide." She held out her hands and disappeared.

"All right, why don't I look up ways to defeat the frog?" asked Mathias.

"You sure you want to do that?" asked Hailey.

"Yeah, the frog wants to hurt you," Madison added.

"Well, we can't just sit here and wait for Isabelle," said Simon. "We've got to do something."

"I'll take out my laptop," said Mathias.

"Don't bother," said Simon. "I've updated my Internet connection, so we can go on my tablet and look up what the frog eats."

"What was wrong with the Internet before?" asked Hailey.

"It was a bit slow," said Simon. "But it's better now." He grabbed his tablet from the couch and picked it up—only for a thump to come from outside.

"The frog couldn't have come here so fast," said Jasmine.

A croak sounded. Everybody turned to the tent flaps.

"Everyone, let's hide now," said Mathias. "I've been thinking that we stay out here, so if something happens to Isabelle, we'll know."

They each put on a poncho. Alyssa sat on the couch, her chest stinging. Prickles tingled under her skin and sweat spotted her face. The thumps and croaks grew louder. Alyssa rushed her breathing. The same noises vibrated her eardrums as they continued to louden. But a swish sounded, and Alyssa gasped. Uh oh. Had the frog appeared under the tent?

The answer was yes. Alyssa leaned back, ready to shriek. She opened her mouth but covered it since she remembered what the creature would do. A frog about the size of a deer looked down. It had a huge black eye in its face's center and slimy-looking brown skin. Alyssa shut her eyes and considered what the frog might do to her.

When is Isabelle going to be back? Alyssa asked herself. She heard no other swishes, and Mathias would refrain from calling Isabelle on his phone right now.

"You are welcome to weaken me," said Mathias in a robotic tone.

Alyssa gasped and opened her eyes. She turned to Mathias, who looked at the frog. His eyes had turned all yellow as if he had no irises or pupils. The frog croaked and stuck out its tongue, which wrapped around Mathias's body and pulled him toward it.

Temptations to remove the poncho took over Alyssa's mind. Her jaw stayed dropped as she quickened up her breaths. Tears watered her eyes as the frog's eye puffed with black gas. The gas clouded around Mathias.

"No!" squeaked Alyssa. But she clapped her hand over her mouth.

"Mathias!" cried Isabelle.

Alyssa turned to her as she staggered down the stairs, carrying a large box. She put it down as the frog let go of him. But the frog looked at her and hypnotized her too.

"I've got to save them," whispered Alyssa. She unzipped her hood and peeled off her poncho.

"Alyssa, what are you doing?" whispered Simon. "Get back here."

"But the frog's hurting Isabelle," said Alyssa.

"It's too late," said Destiny.

"What?" Alyssa turned to Isabelle and Mathias. Both lay on the ground and moved nothing. The frog shut its eye and disappeared.

"What happened?" shrieked Hailey.

"The frog weakened us." Isabelle lifted her head up.

"We won't be able to help you anymore," said Mathias.

"Are you serious?" asked Hailey.

"Yes," said Mathias.

14

About a half hour ago, the girls had carried Isabelle and Mathias to their bed. Isabelle had also told Alyssa to call a doctor from Kipling's Hospital to come for both her and Mathias. According to Isabelle, wizard doctors could see two patients at one time during emergencies. Unlike the ordinary culture Alyssa had grown up in, magician doctors could also visit patients if they had time.

Any moment, a doctor from Kipling's Hospital would appear inside the tent. Alyssa hoped that he could cure Isabelle's and Mathias's weaknesses. She sat on her bed and tapped the mattress. The other girls did the same. Hailey and Madison joined Alyssa, while Jasmine and Destiny sat on the middle bed.

A swish suggested to Alyssa that the doctor had arrived. She turned to the door and watched him carry a small briefcase here. He introduced himself with an Indian accent.

"Hi." Isabelle lay on her bed with Mathias.

"Do you want the girls out while I'm here?" asked the doctor.

"They can stay," said Mathias. "I'm totally cool with it."

"Okay." The doctor walked toward their bed.

He asked Mathias and Isabelle how they had lost their strength, and they answered. Then he put a patch on each right arm and whipped his wand at it. It turned golden yellow with black polka dots.

"Okay, you two have Zooaefortus," he said.

"What is that?" asked Madison.

"It's a magical weakness caused by animals," The doctor turned back to Isabelle and Mathias. "And if the animal's brain was dominated by something manmade, you can't cure the weakness or retrieve your magical skills."

"Why not?" asked Isabelle.

"No one has been able to find a cure for it," said the doctor. "But you'll be able to get your strength and magical skills back if and only if the person who owned that computer dies. For now, I'll make you a walker to help you walk when you need to use the bathroom or get up for anything." He created two walkers with his wand.

"Thank you," said Mathias.

"We're going to have to find a way to kill him," said Isabelle. "Girls, tonight you and Simon should brainstorm ways to defeat Master Beau. Also—make sure they're all indirect, meaning he can't see you hurt him."

"Why?" asked Destiny.

"You don't want Master Beau to catch you," said Isabelle. "Plus, you're not old enough to use anything dangerous."

"Sounds like a plan," said Jasmine. "Where's Simon?"

"I'm in the kitchen," he said.

"Can you come out here?" shouted Isabelle.

Simon appeared in the bedroom. Isabelle repeated to him what she'd told the girls.

"I'll do that now," he said. "Let's go into the living room, girls. We should let Isabelle and Mathias rest."

Everyone sat as Simon turned on his tablet.

"Now, girls, before we think of ways to hurt Master Beau, I need to see what he's up to right now," said Simon. "I also want to make sure he didn't make any changes to anything inside the center."

The girls gathered around him to view Master Beau on the screen.

Master Beau sat in his office and typed on his laptop. Someone knocked on the door.

"Come in," he said.

The door opened to reveal David. "Hello, Master Beau."

"Hi. I'm impressed that your progress is getting better."

"Thank you. I came here to ask why you put a bulb on the door to the computer room."

"I don't want any unauthorized people going in there. If someone who doesn't work here tries to go in there alone, the alarm will go off, and I'll kick that person out. Do you have any other questions?"

"No."

"Okay then. You can get back to work."

David left.

"Well, that's great," said Simon. "Now we're going to have to find another way to hurt him."

"How about we give him some potion—"

"We can't buy dangerous potions without a license, Madison," said Simon.

"Can you create your own?" Madison asked.

"Nope," said Simon. "You can't create harmful substances with magic, especially ones that can hurt or kill you."

"I hope he's allergic to something," said Destiny.

"I wouldn't rely on that," said Simon.

"Aw, darn it." Destiny crossed her arms.

"I have an idea," said Alyssa. "Why don't we fool him into thinking something's dangerous, and when he gets there, something will happen to him?"

"What did you have in mind?" Jasmine asked.

"Um . . . we'd play a recording of one of his workers in danger, and when he gets there, we'd have sleeping gas to knock him out. Then we'd inject water into his arm, and he'll die."

"How do you know all this?" Madison asked. "We never learned about that in science."

"My uncle once played the news in the car, and there was a story where that happened," said Alyssa.

"I'm not sure about the recording part, although I really like that idea," said Simon.

"What's wrong with the recording part?" asked Alyssa.

"I don't have any ways to capture any of his workers' voices," said Simon.

"So what can we do, Simon?" asked Alyssa.

"Tonight, while I'm sleeping, I'll absorb what types of entertainment he likes. We'll play something loud so that he can hear it."

"That sounds good," said Alyssa.

"All right, so tomorrow let's all wake up by seven-thirty, and we'll do this," said Simon.

*   *   *   *

The next morning, Simon served Isabelle and Mathias some fruit and cereal since he couldn't create hot cooked food. He created the same things for the girls.

"Why can't you create pancakes, waffles, French toast—stuff like that?" asked Destiny.

"I don't have that skill," said Simon. "You're going to have to deal with what I can make."

"You can't even cook?" asked Destiny.

"Just eat what you have," said Simon. "We want to get out as soon as possible so that Master Beau can die and Isabelle and Mathias can be strong again."

"What kind of entertainment does Master Beau like?" asked Madison.

"Ah, thanks for asking, Madison," said Simon. "He likes jazz music a lot."

"Do you have that on your WiPod?" asked Hailey.

"Uh huh," said Simon.

After breakfast, Simon grabbed his WiPod from the bedroom.

Isabelle lifted her head up. "You really think your plan's a good idea, Simon?"

"It was Alyssa's idea," he said.

Mathias and Isabelle turned to Alyssa as she stood by her and Hailey's bed.

"I actually like that idea," said Simon. "You said it had to be indirect anyway."

"Well, injecting distilled water is kind of direct." Jasmine stood by her and Madison's bed.

"But he'll be sleeping, so he won't be aware of the needle coming," Simon said.

"Do you have any needles?" asked Alyssa.

"Not right now, but you can make those appear," said Simon. "All right, girls, let's go."

"Wait," said Isabelle. "You don't have anything that can take you there."

"You've got a point," said Simon.

"Don't give up, though," said Mathias. "I have an idea."

"What is it?" asked Simon.

"Why don't you program yourself into the tracking app on your tablet and let the girls watch you there?" asked Mathias. "You don't want them near Master Beau anyway."

"You do have a point," said Simon. "All right—I'll do that." He grabbed his tablet from the living room and flew back into the bedroom, where he tapped different parts of the screen. He landed and said, "Okay, I did it. I programmed the tracking app to track me."

"Great." Mathias smiled.

"Okay, girls, I'm going to disappear to the dark magic center," said Simon. "Please watch me so that you can see what I'm doing."

Alyssa and the other girls nodded.

Simon grabbed his WiPod and an invisibility poncho, made his speakers and some sleeping gas appear, and then disappeared.

"Do you guys want to watch too?" Alyssa asked Mathias and Isabelle.

"Sure," said Mathias.

Alyssa placed the tablet on the nightstand next to Mathias and Isabelle and leaned it against the wall. She then unlocked it, pressed the spy icon, selected Simon as the tracking choice, and then chose the video option to see him. Simon set everything up.

"Do we have to watch this?" asked Destiny. "Watching Simon set up is such a waste of time."

"Shut up, Destiny," said Hailey.

Then jazz music blasted.

"Look—the music's playing," said Madison.

Alyssa turned to the screen and saw Simon put his poncho on while the music played. Master Beau hadn't come out. After three minutes, though, he opened the building's front door.

"What's this music playing?" he exclaimed. He disappeared and appeared outside of the fence surrounding the building. "Whoever's playing it, either you shut it off, or I will destroy whatever device it's coming from!" He looked down at the can of sleeping gas. "Oh no, not a prank." He whipped his wand at it, and it disappeared.

Simon turned and gasped. He shut off his music and grabbed his WiPod and speakers.

"Whoever's responsible for this—show yourself!" Master Beau screamed.

Simon pushed himself up, still wearing his poncho. He carried everything as he flew away.

"I think I saw some white marble above me," said Master Beau. "I suspect it's someone helping Alyssa and her friends."

Alyssa inhaled and experienced tingling. Master Beau couldn't catch Simon and harm him. But he pointed his wand at Simon's foot and blew the poncho off him.

"Come with me!" Master Beau pointed his wand at Simon. A spark shot out and forced Simon to the ground.

"You won't be able to disappear or fly anymore." Master Beau picked up Simon.

"Hey, put me down!" yelled Simon. "My WiPod's still on the ground!"

"You won't be needing it anymore," said Master Beau. "I'm going to do something to you that'll shock the girls."

15

"What are we going to do?" whined Hailey. "I don't want anything to happen to Simon!"

"We've got to do something," said Alyssa.

"I don't think there's anything we can do," said Jasmine.

"Well, we can't just let Master Beau hurt Simon." Alyssa turned to Isabelle. "Isabelle, do you have a private taxi driver?"

"I do, but he can't drive to the dark magic center. There are no roads leading to it."

"So we have to let him go?" squeaked Alyssa, tears stinging her eyes.

"Alyssa, don't get upset," said Mathias. "We'll call the police."

"But Master Beau's invisible to the police," Alyssa said. "So is the center." She turned around, covering her face as tears trickled down. Some even poured onto her striped shirt's U-neck.

"There's got to be something," wept Hailey.

"I have an idea," said Isabelle.

"What?" asked Hailey.

"You can call my pilot," Isabelle said.

Hailey picked up the phone and looked at it. "How do you turn it on?"

"Press the round button on the bottom," said Isabelle.

Hailey did so, but nothing happened. "It's not turning on."

"I guess it's out of charge," said Isabelle.

"Take my phone," said Mathias. "It's an Endroid, the magical version of the Android, so it may work a little differently."

"How?" asked Hailey.

"You turn it on at the top," Mathias said.

Hailey nodded and picked up the other phone. She pressed the button on top—it did nothing.

"This stinks," said Hailey.

"I guess it's time for plan B," said Alyssa.

Everyone looked at her.

"What's plan B?" asked Madison.

"We're going to have to walk there ourselves," said Alyssa.

"Are you crazy?" asked Jasmine.

"Yeah, Alyssa, that's the dumbest plan I've ever heard," said Destiny.

"Look, Simon's in trouble, and if we don't try and save him—we might never be able to go back home again."

"He already can't fly or disappear," said Destiny. "I can't imagine that he'll be able to help us."

"Well, we still can't let him suffer." Alyssa picked up his tablet and unlocked it. He was already at the center, according to the map. But he didn't move.

"What happened to Simon?" asked Hailey.

"The dot of him isn't moving," replied Alyssa.

"Open the video option," said Madison.

"How?" asked Alyssa.

"Do you remember how Simon did it?" Jasmine asked.

"Um . . . not really," said Alyssa.

"Well, that's just great," said Destiny.

"Hey—this is a magic tablet," Alyssa said. "I'm not going to be an expert on this."

"Alyssa, can we go now?" asked Hailey.

"Yes, let's go," said Alyssa.

"Alyssa, I don't think you'll be able to walk there," said Isabelle.

"Yeah, it's too far of a walk," Mathias added. "I don't want anything to happen to you guys."

"I think they're right," said Jasmine. "We can't walk there."

"Well, if someone's in trouble, we sometimes have to take risks," said Alyssa. "You see that in movies a lot."

"Well, Alyssa, movies aren't like real life," Jasmine said.

"So?" she asked. "At least they teach you a lesson, and I bet a common one is that if someone you love is in trouble, you've got to risk everything you can do to save them."

A few swishes suggested to Alyssa that some people had appeared. She turned around, seeing David, Clarissa, Seamus, and Master Beau.

"What did you do with Simon?" shrieked Hailey.

"You want to see?" asked Master Beau.

"Let him go!" yelled Alyssa.

"Never," said Master Beau. "He's frozen."

Everyone gasped.

"No!" squeaked Hailey.

Master Beau took out his tablet and showed the girls a picture of Simon. He'd turned icy blue and stood with his mouth open. Tears watered Alyssa's eyes. She turned away, smearing her tears out of her eyes. The other girls cried too.

"Oh my goodness, y'all," said Clarissa. "Can you stop crying?"

"Unfreeze him!" wailed Hailey.

"No!" snapped Master Beau.

"Get out of here!" exclaimed Mathias.

"You're too weak to fight!" yelled Seamus.

David whispered in Seamus's ear, and he nodded. Then the two men pointed their wands at Isabelle and Mathias.

"What are you doing?" squealed Alyssa.

"*Somnum harena!*" they bellowed.

The sand propelled itself into Isabelle's and Mathias's eyes and knocked them out.

"No!" screamed Alyssa.

"They wouldn't have been able to protect you anyway!" yelled David.

"Just get out of here!" squawked Hailey.

"No!" Master Beau held his wand out. "*Somnum harena!*"

"No—Hailey!" yelled Alyssa as the sand knocked Hailey out.

"Quiet, McCarthy!" Master Beau pointed his wand at her. "You're actually next!"

"Don't—"

"*Somnum harena!*" roared Master Beau.

Alyssa backed away as the sand swirled toward her. It propelled into her eyelids, and she whined through gritted teeth—until her energy levels dropped and she collapsed.

*   *   *   *

A plant scent drifted into Alyssa's nostrils. She inhaled it through her nose and blinked. Master Beau stood over her and blocked the damp gray ceiling. Alyssa could feel cuffs squeeze her wrists and ankles and chains that connected them to the wall.

"All right, I've woken all of you up," said Master Beau.

Alyssa gasped at how far away the bars stood since the last time she'd come here to rescue the other girls. They seemed several more feet away.

"What happened?" asked Hailey.

"After I knocked you all out, a few other workers came here with stretchers and flew you here in the tubes parked outside of your tent," said Master Beau

"You stole our mentors' tubes?" screeched Hailey.

"Yes," said Master Beau.

"You monster!" exclaimed Alyssa.

"Quiet!" Master Beau snapped.

"What happened to this place?" asked Madison.

"I extended it," said Master Beau. "Because the frog, unfortunately, died, one of my workers brought another creature here and should be here soon with it."

"What's it going to do?" asked Madison.

"Kill you—and your friends."

"No!" squeaked Hailey.

"Let us out!" cried Alyssa.

"Shut up!" said Master Beau.

Someone knocked on the door.

"I'll be right there!" Master Beau rushed to answer it. David stood outside, holding a leash.

"Ah, perfect—you brought the centidile." Master Beau stuck his head outside the door opening.

"It was no problem," said David.

"Well, I'm going to have to take the muzzle off so that it can bite the girls," Master Beau said.

"Yeah, of course," David said.

Master Beau took the leash. "I'll take it from here. Thank you."

"You're welcome." David left.

Alyssa's chest stung, and her heart palpitated all over her body as Master Beau pulled the leash. She couldn't believe it—her life would end soon. No way could she bid goodbye to the world and forget about seeing everyone at home again. Thoughts of dying forced tears into her eyes and then out to pour down her cheeks.

A snout covered by a muzzle showed itself—followed by its head and then its feet. It looked like a regular crocodile but this one had two feet on either side of its body. One at the side and one below its belly. Its height still matched that of an ordinary crocodile, but the length of its body didn't end.

"Girls, this is a centidile—a crocodile with a hundred legs." Master Beau led it toward the bars. "It will be the last thing you'll ever see."

"Please—let us go!" wailed Hailey.

"We don't want to die!" sobbed Madison.

"Yeah, please!" said Alyssa.

"Too late." Master Beau took the muzzle off the centidile. He unlocked the button's cover and pressed it. As the bars rose, he unleashed the centidile. It crawled past the bars. "It's going to bite you for ten seconds," said Master Beau. "During that time, your life will fade, and then you'll be dead." He pressed the button again, and the bars lowered.

"What do we do?" squealed Hailey.

The centidile crawled toward her and snapped its snout. Everyone screamed, trying to move away as much as possible. The centidile approached Hailey and aimed its snout toward her leg.

"Kick it!" bellowed Alyssa. "Now!"

Hailey kicked its snout—but it snapped again.

"Keep kicking it until its nose bleeds!" shouted Madison.

"Okay!" Hailey continued to hurt the centidile—until it bit her. "Ow!" she cried.

"I know what to do!" Destiny kicked the centidile and caused it to release Hailey's leg. Hailey looked down and gasped at the blood spilling out.

"How'd you do that?" Alyssa exclaimed.

"I've practiced over the years!" yelled Destiny.

Alyssa knew it'd come from bullying.

"So let's all kick it until it dies!" said Destiny.

But the centidile snapped at her and sank its teeth into her leg.

"Punch it, Destiny!" yelped Alyssa. "Be a bully to it!"

But she gasped, and her energy faded.

"Destiny, no!" howled Jasmine. "You can't give up!"

Her eyes shut, and her breathing slowed down—until the centidile slid out. Destiny woke up and gasped, and a bird cawed.

"Regulus!" Alyssa turned to him.

His claws had sunk into the creature's tail. It snapped at him, but he bit its nose—and kept his beak there.

Alyssa turned away as blood poured out from the centidile's nose. After many seconds, she turned back. The centidile lay motionless on the floor. Regulus trotted toward Alyssa and the others. He leaned down near Alyssa and bit her cuff. She gasped until he broke it. "Thanks," she panted.

Regulus broke her other cuff and repeated the same thing with everybody else.

"How are you going to get us out, Regulus?" asked Alyssa.

His band formed words.

I have the ability to create holes in ceilings. Is this the highest floor?

Alyssa nodded.

Perfect. By the way, Simon the marble figure had sent me a message that you and your friends were in danger here. Marble figures can still do that while they're frozen. It's also the only magical skill that can't lose at all.

"Alyssa, what are you doing?" squeaked Jasmine. "We need to get out of here!"

"Climb onto this creature!" Alyssa climbed onto Regulus's back after he leaned his head down.

"Alyssa, are you crazy?" asked Jasmine.

"This creature is the only one who can help us get out!" Alyssa said. "Climb on before Master Beau catches us!"

Regulus knelt, and the girls climbed onto him. He looked up at the ceiling. It shook as if an earthquake occurred. Alyssa held onto his neck, and Hailey wrapped her arm around her body.

"What's going on?" Master Beau thundered from outside of the room.

Alyssa gasped, turning to the door. She looked back at the ceiling and saw it crack. More and more cracks formed until the ceiling opened.

"Hold on, guys!" exclaimed Alyssa.

Regulus lifted his front feet up and flapped his wings. He pushed himself up and soared out of the building. Everyone except Alyssa screamed as he straightened his body. He flew away from the dark magic center. However, his band had never told her where he would take Alyssa and the others.

Approaching the beach, Regulus flew straight. He passed the shore and ocean.

"Hey, he missed the beach!" screamed Madison.

Alyssa wondered if Regulus would take the girls to Dermand Island.

16

A small island, probably Dermand Island, came closer into Alyssa's sight as Regulus flew toward it. He tilted forward and descended to the island.

"Alyssa, what's going on?" bellowed Hailey.

"I'm not sure!"

"Why aren't we going back to where the tent is?" screamed Jasmine.

"I said I don't know!" yelled Alyssa.

Regulus's front feet touched the ground, followed by his back feet. He trotted along the shore, and the girls bumped up and down on his back. He slowed down and stopped. Then he leaned his head down.

"Let's go, guys," said Alyssa.

"Alyssa, you've got to be kidding me," said Destiny. "I'm not getting off here."

"Come on." Alyssa slid off Regulus's back. "There's got to be a reason why we're here."

Regulus's band formed words.

I have taken you back to Dermand Island because Rosaline and Penelope have actually discovered something that can indirectly kill anyone who is threatening them.

"Really?" asked Alyssa.

Yes. However, it'll only work if you can think of a good memory.

"Guys, get off him now," said Alyssa. "I just found out why we're here."

"How could you possibly have found out?" Destiny asked.

"This creature's wearing a band on his leg," Alyssa said.

"What is this animal, anyway?" asked Jasmine.

"A marshakeet, half lorikeet and half kangaroo." Alyssa noticed words forming on Regulus's band.

I am going to send signals to Rosaline and Penelope. Tell the other girls not to bother me while I shut my eyes and focus.

"Okay, guys, let's leave him alone." Alyssa looked up at the others.

"What were you reading?" Hailey asked.

Alyssa told them about the band.

"What's a dermaiden?" asked Madison.

"Half woman and half dolphin," Alyssa answered. "Now let's walk away." She led the other girls away from Regulus.

"What are we going to do now?" asked Hailey.

Alyssa summarized the instructions from Regulus's band.

"How are we going to do that?" asked Jasmine.

Two familiar voices singing the tune of "My Heart Will Go On" from *Titanic* attracted the girls' attention. Alyssa turned to the ocean as the voices grew louder.

"How do they know that song?" Jasmine asked.

Alyssa answered, and the song ended. Flukes flapped against the surface of the water. Rosaline and Penelope popped their heads up. All the girls except Alyssa gasped.

"I don't believe it," said Jasmine.

"Me either," said Madison.

"Hey, guys," Alyssa said to Rosaline and Penelope.

Rosaline created the same smoke-filled glass cube from last time and handed that to Alyssa. Then she spoke her native dermaiden language, and the words appeared inside the glass.

Penelope and I have the seashells you'll need to defeat whoever's after you. They are in the pouches in our tails. We'll get them out now.

The two reached into their tails' pouches and pulled out the seashells.

"Thank you," said Alyssa. "Come on, guys, let's take them."

Each girl took one seashell and put it in her shorts pocket.

"How did you get pouches?" Alyssa asked Rosaline and Penelope.

Rosaline spoke, and the words spelled out inside the cube.

Our father gave us these when we received Regulus's message about you being hunted down.

"Cool," said Alyssa.
Then Penelope spoke and made her words spell out into the cube.

Rosaline and I need to go since we don't want to get hurt in case whoever's hunting you down sees us. We'll be back after we see that you've defeated your enemies.

The dermaidens swam away, and Alyssa waved goodbye to them. Regulus walked up to her with words on his band.

I'm not impervious to magic, unlike most magical creatures, so I am going to fly away until Rosaline and Penelope find out that you've defeated the villains. Good luck.

Alyssa sighed. "Fine."
Regulus trotted away from her and the other girls and took off. Alyssa stared at him until he flew too far away.
"All right, guys, let's start now," Alyssa turned to them.
"There they are!" roared David.
Alyssa and the others gasped. David, Seamus, Clarissa, and Master Beau had appeared here.
"You may have escaped from the prison room, but that doesn't mean we're giving up!" growled Master Beau.
"If you're wondering why we're here now, it's because Master Beau's laptop, which has a tracking program to track y'all, had a problem," Clarissa said. "But now it's fixed, and we found you."
"Clarissa, you didn't have to tell them that," said Seamus.
"All right, guys, that's enough," Master Beau said. "Seamus, can you make the minute vase appear?"
"Yes, sir." He held out his arms and made a vase filled with water appear. Then he handed it to Master Beau.
"Okay, girls, here's how it works," said Master Beau. "The water will fog and eventually turn white like milk. While that happens, you will lose your strength and weaken until you die. That'll happen when the water turns white."
"Why didn't you buy it before?" Clarissa asked.

"It wasn't available anywhere until today," Master Beau put it down and whipped his wand at it. Fog clouded the water, and the girls inhaled.

"Let's run," said Alyssa. She and the other girls dashed, but her legs ached, and she slowed down. The same thing happened with the other kids, and each one dropped to her knees and then hands. Alyssa gasped and panted while her arms shook.

"That's right, get weaker," said Master Beau. "In thirty seconds, you'll be dead."

Alyssa's arms dropped, and her eyes drooped. She breathed more and relaxed herself—but remembered that she and the others needed to think of good memories.

"Guys, h-hurry and think of something g-good you remember," Alyssa whispered.

She shut her eyes and slowed down her breathing. With few seconds left to live, she thought about what it'd be like to be dead. No—she shouldn't. She had to think of a *good* memory.

The first image that came to her mind was a tin of decorated sugar cookies. Right—Aunt Laura had baked those. Then Aunt Laura came to her mind—which led to the Christmas of 2005, when Aunt Laura had made cookies. Alyssa managed to get a picture of that time in her head.

Although death drew nearer to her, she still heard a laser shooting out of the seashell in her shorts pocket—followed by screaming and a thump on the ground. She lifted her head up and opened her eyes. She gasped and pushed herself up. But the other girls still lay on the ground. Tears watered Alyssa's eyes—until they too gasped and pushed themselves up.

"Oh my god, we're okay!" cried Madison.

Alyssa turned to Master Beau, who lay on the ground.

"You killed him." David turned to Alyssa.

"Look, the water in the vase is gone," Seamus said.

"That's what's supposed to happen, Seamus," said David. "You need to read more."

"Shut up," said Seamus, his voice breaking.

Alyssa looked at Hailey, Madison, Jasmine, and Destiny, who all had their eyes shut. Green lasers shot out of their shorts-pockets (except for Destiny), and hit David, Seamus, and Clarissa. They screamed and then fell to the ground. The girls stared and breathed.

"We did it," said Madison. "We're safe."

"But how are we going to let the dermaidens know?" asked Jasmine.

A caw grew louder from the sky. The girls looked up and saw Regulus flying toward them.

"Regulus," said Alyssa.

He lowered toward the island and landed. He trotted to the girls, and Alyssa saw words form on his band.

Congratulations on defeating your enemies. Rosaline and Penelope will come soon so that you can return the seashells.

"How'd you know to come?" asked Jasmine.

When those seashells defeat someone evil, the magic in the lasers sends signals to whoever owns them and lets them know what happened. After Rosaline and Penelope found out, they sent a signal to me to tell me to come here.

"Are you going to take us back to the tent?" asked Jasmine.

Yes—but after you return the seashells to Rosaline and Penelope.

Alyssa turned to the ocean, where Rosaline and Penelope singing the tune of "Seasons of Love" from *Rent* ascended. Their flukes churned the water as they came closer. When their song ended, they popped their heads out of the water and held their hands out. Each girl returned her seashell to Penelope or Rosaline. Then Rosaline created the cube and gave it to Alyssa. She spoke, and Alyssa looked into the cube.

Great job on defeating the villains. Now hop onto Regulus's back, and he'll take you back to wherever you're staying.

"Okay," said Alyssa.

Rosaline spoke again.

If you're able to go home, I want to wish you a safe trip. Now it's time to say goodbye.

Alyssa handed the cube back to Rosaline and said, "Thank you for everything."

The dermaidens waved and swam away. Alyssa turned to Regulus, who placed his head on the ground.

"Let's go, guys," Alyssa told the others.

She climbed onto him, and he knelt so that the other girls could climb onto his back too. After they all did that, he stood up, trotted, and took flight.

17

Regulus landed on the beach where the tent stood, and he trotted toward it. He then slowed down and stopped to let everyone off. He placed his head on the ground, and Alyssa slid off him. The other girls got off, and Regulus lifted his head up.

Alyssa petted his feathery neck. "Thanks, Regulus. I couldn't have won without you."

Regulus's eyes watered.

"Goodbye." Alyssa removed her hand from him, and he trotted away from her. He flew away, and Alyssa sprinted into the tent and down into the living room, where Mathias, Simon, and Isabelle stood.

"Blimey, you did it." Simon smiled.

"We're so proud of you girls," said Mathias.

"Thanks." Alyssa grinned.

"How'd you defeat Master Beau?" Isabelle asked.

Alyssa explained everything from the time Regulus had rescued her and the other girls from the dark magic center to when Master Beau and his three favorite workers had died.

"Wow, that's incredible," said Isabelle.

"I was so happy when my body unfroze and I then flew and disappeared back here," said Simon.

"Did you ever get your WiPod back?" Madison asked.

"Sadly, no." Simon frowned. "But I do have everything backed up on my laptop, which I left at home. So when I do get a new one, I don't have to buy everything all over again."

"Great," said Madison.

"What's going to happen with the dark magic center now that the charms are gone?" asked Alyssa.

"I'm going to report them," said Mathias.

"Why don't you do that later?" asked Isabelle. "We should work on getting these girls home."

"Isabelle, you can call your pilot and see if he's available," Mathias told her. "And if you could go—"

"Why do you need—?" Isabelle sighed. "You're right. Go ahead and report that place wherever you're comfortable."

"Thanks." Mathias walked into the bedroom, and Isabelle made her cell phone appear. She pressed her device's screen and held it to her ear. Alyssa sat down on the wide couch and watched Isabelle greet her private pilot.

"When are you next available?" she asked over the phone.

Alyssa continued to watch to find out an answer.

"I need to send five girls to New Jersey. How is this all going to work?"

A long pause occurred. Alyssa assumed that the pilot had to provide lots of details.

"Okay, thanks. See you tonight. Bye." Isabelle hung up. "All right, girls, my pilot will be here at midnight. Now here's how it's going to work. When you get back to the United States, you won't be going directly home."

"Why not?" asked Hailey.

"Because you technically entered this country illegally, even though it wasn't your fault," Isabelle said.

"So where will we be going?" asked Hailey.

"To a magical immigration center called Griffin Immigration Center for Magical Travel," replied Isabelle. "It's not far from you guys. It's in the Bronx."

"What are we going to do there?" asked Hailey.

"Well, Mathias is going to write a note that proves you were kidnapped. The person at the front desk will run it through a truth-detecting machine. After they find out that the note is true, you'll all get wristbands to wear to confirm that you were kidnapped. But because you are all underage and will be unaccompanied, you'll have to have attendants escort you through the process."

"You're not coming with us?" asked Madison.

"Sorry, no," said Isabelle. "Also, you're going to have to deal with being jetlagged. People aren't allowed to bring potions when they travel."

"Not even in their luggage?" asked Madison.

"Nope," Isabelle said. "It can be dangerous. So you're going to have to let your mind adjust to the Eastern Time Zone naturally."

"Okay," said Madison.

"That's fine," said Alyssa.

"All right, guys, the police are on their way to the dark magic center." Mathias walked out of the bedroom.

"Good to hear," said Isabelle. "Can you write a note explaining that the girls were kidnapped?"

"Why?" asked Mathias.

Isabelle told him the same thing she'd told them.

"Okay." Mathias turned to Simon. "You should return your tracking app now."

"I'll do that." Simon made his tablet appear and worked on returning the tracking app.

"Should we go pack now?" asked Madison.

"Yes," said Mathias. "I'll go write the note in the meantime."

*   *   *   *

Someone knocked on the bedroom door, and Alyssa bolted upright from her bed. She and the other girls had slept since nine p.m. Opening the door, she saw a tall black man standing next to Isabelle. He introduced himself to her.

"Can you wake the other girls up?" he asked.

Alyssa nodded and did so.

As the other girls woke up, Isabelle strode over to Alyssa. "Are you turning thirteen soon?"

"Yeah, next month," said Alyssa.

"What day?" asked Isabelle.

"The seventeenth," Alyssa replied. "Why?"

"There's something important I need to give you, but I have to wait until you're thirteen."

"How come?" asked Alyssa.

"The magic in this object can be harmful to children under thirteen," said Isabelle.

"What is the object?" Alyssa asked.

"Alyssa, time to go!" Hailey called.

"You should get going, Alyssa," said Isabelle. "You'll find out more about the object once we can travel to America and when you're thirteen."

"Okay." Alyssa nodded. She picked up her backpack, grabbed her suitcase, and walked toward where the girls stood.

"Do you want to take out something long sleeved?" the pilot asked.

"Right," said Alyssa. "It's still cold in New Jersey." She took out a hoodie from her suitcase. Her long coral T-shirt wouldn't be enough to wear in whatever weather New Jersey experienced now.

"Do you have the note?" Madison asked the pilot.

"Yep," he answered. "Now are we all ready to go?"

The girls said that they were.

After bidding goodbye to Isabelle, Mathias, and Simon, the girls hopped into the back seat of the pilot's helicopter. Alyssa took out a hairbrush to brush her tresses.

"Are we going to go through a portal?" asked Hailey.

"In two hours," said the pilot. "When we arrive at the immigration center, it'll be six p.m., Thursday."

*   *   *   *

The helicopter stopped. Alyssa opened her eyes and saw a pink sunset spread across the sky. She also spotted dead trees, pines, and people walking across the terminal in jackets. At last— she'd returned to the United States.

"Okay, girls, rise and shine," the pilot said. "We're at the immigration center."

Everyone stretched, yawned, and moaned. Alyssa put her hoodie on and zipped it halfway up her shirt. She also thanked herself for wearing leggings instead of shorts before she'd left Fiji.

The pilot escorted the girls to the front desk outside of the entrance, where a frowning man sat.

"Please show proof that they're here legally," the guy behind the desk said.

The pilot took out Mathias's note and handed it to him. He scanned it through what looked like a regular computer scanner. The process included a soft buzz, which went on for about ten seconds. Then a ding occurred, along with a green light in the button at the top of the scanner.

"You're good," said the man. "Are they all unaccompanied?"

"Yes," answered the pilot.

"Okay, I'm going to need their wrists for the wristbands." The man then explained what they were for.

Alyssa held out her arm first. The man wrapped a red wristband around it. He repeated the same step for the other girls. Then he spoke into his walkie-talkie, telling somebody about five unaccompanied minors.

"You'll be getting some attendants in a few minutes." The man put his walkie-talkie down. "Please stay here while you wait."

"You want me to stay with them?" asked the pilot.

"Yes," answered the man.

After about two or three minutes, five people in blue-and-black uniforms came out. The man at the front assigned a different one to each girl.

"We'll take them from here," said Alyssa's attendant, a short-haired Asian woman.

"Okay," said the pilot "Bye, girls."

"Bye," the girls said.

He climbed back into his helicopter and took off.

"So where are we going now?" Alyssa asked her attendant.

"Through immigrations and customs," she responded. "It's the same as going through them at a regular airport."

"No one has any potions or magical items, right?" asked Hailey's attendant.

The girls shook their heads.

Alyssa hadn't gone through immigrations and customs since she and the Flynns had traveled to the Cayman Islands during the Christmas vacation of 2006. She hadn't remembered much of that, but as she went through the same processes here at Griffin's, the actions taken set off an alarm inside her head. She appreciated how the lines had few people, because she longed to go home and lie down.

Several minutes of going through immigrations and customs had passed, and the attendants led the girls into the pickup terminal. Unlike regular airports, this one had fewer baggage claim carousels. The girls already had their bags, but Alyssa still tilted her head at the carousels.

"What's with the carousels?" asked Hailey. "Why aren't there that many?"

"Because this isn't as busy as an ordinary airport," answered Hailey's attendant.

"Okay, girls, listen up," said Madison's attendant. "Because you are all unaccompanied minors, we have to drive you back to your houses."

"How come?" asked Madison.

"Because we can't trust taxis to drive you home," answered her attendant. "It's our policy. Even regular airports don't allow people to accept unsolicited rides."

"We can't have our parents pick us up?" asked Madison.

"You can if you think they won't mind driving all the way from New Jersey," Madison's attendant said. "It's quite a drive."

"How long from Bursnell?" asked Madison.

"About two and a half hours," her attendant replied.

"You can take us," Madison said.

"I'll take you to my car," Madison's attendant said.

Madison, Destiny, and Jasmine walked with their attendants out the door.

"Are you ready to go, Alyssa?" asked Alyssa's attendant.

"Same here, Hailey?" Hailey's attendant checked.

"We live together," said Hailey.

"So we'll all be traveling in one car?" Hailey's attendant asked Alyssa's attendant.

"Yeah, that's a good idea." She nodded.

Alyssa and Hailey followed their attendants to the parking lot.

"Do you want to take your car?" Alyssa's attendant asked Hailey's attendant.

"Sure. Where are we going?" She sat in the driver's seat.

"Forty Cygnus Lane, Opal Stream, New Jersey," said Hailey. Her attendant programmed that address into the GPS.

"Do you two have cell phones?" asked Hailey's attendant.

"No," Alyssa and Hailey said.

"We'll let you borrow ours then." Alyssa's attendant reached into her pants pocket. "Another rule for unaccompanied minors is that when they arrive home, there must be a trustworthy adult in the house."

"What if there isn't?" asked Hailey.

"Then we have to wait with you until they come home," answered her attendant. "If it's not for a while, we take you back here and wait until they're home."

"They should be home," said Hailey.

"Just make sure they'll be there within a couple of hours." Hailey's attendant handed her the phone. Then she backed out and drove.

Alyssa's attendant also handed her a phone. Hailey told Alyssa Donald's number because she called Kathleen. After dialing Donald's number, Alyssa put the device to her ear and listened to the ringing.

"Hello?" Donald answered.

"Hey, Donald, it's Alyssa."

"Oh my goodness, what happened?" he cried. "First, Kathleen and I couldn't find you, and then some jerk kidnapped Hailey!"

"I'll tell you what happened." Alyssa told him everything relevant from the time Master Beau had kidnapped her up until now.

"I can't believe you're okay," said Donald.

"Yeah," said Alyssa.

"Well, we'll have something special for you when you get home, kiddo," Donald said.

"Thank you," yawned Alyssa. "Bye." She gave the phone back to her attendant and lay back in her seat, shutting her eyes.

The GPS's voice and the car's engine turning off let Alyssa know that the attendants had stopped at Kathleen and Donald's house.

"Okay, girls, wake up," said Hailey's attendant. "We're here."

Alyssa opened her eyes and stretched. She turned to her window and looked at a brick house similar her old one, except that this had a garden lined up against it. The garage was also a separate building.

Kathleen opened the drapes in a window next to the door and peeked at them. Hailey and Alyssa waved at her. Then she and Donald rushed out to the car.

"Hey, girls, it's so great to see you," said Kathleen.

Alyssa and Hailey greeted her back.

"Thank you for driving them," Kathleen said to the attendants.

"You're welcome," said the driver.

"How much do we owe?" Donald asked.

"Five hundred dollars," the driver replied.

Kathleen and Donald frowned.

"That much?" asked Donald.

"Donald, it's fine," said Kathleen. "Go get your credit card."

After Donald paid the attendants, he and Kathleen took Alyssa and Hailey inside. Pictures of Uncle Bruce in his youth and Kathleen and Donald covered the walls. A tank of fish rested on a stand in the living room. Alyssa had never found pet fish interesting, but she wished that she'd had an animal back at her old house. Before her parents had died, she'd had a rabbit from when she was four up until she'd started second grade.

Following Kathleen and Donald into the kitchen, Alyssa noticed a pizza box, a Coke bottle, and a jug of lemonade sitting on the table. A tin of snickerdoodle cookies lay on top of the stove.

"Welcome back, girls," said Kathleen. "Have some food."

"You don't want us to unpack first?" Alyssa asked.

"You can unpack later," said Kathleen. "Just lean your stuff against that wall."

Alyssa and Hailey took Kathleen's suggestion. Then they sat down and helped themselves to pizza and drinks.

"So where *were* you guys?" asked Donald.

"Fiji Islands," answered Alyssa.

"You have no idea how worried we were about you, Alyssa," said Donald. "We called the police, we called the missing children's center—we even put up flyers around town with pictures of you and Hailey. I can't believe you two ended up in the Fiji Islands."

"But we did tell the police that you returned here safely," Kathleen added.

"Where'd you find the pictures?" asked Hailey. "We haven't gotten any taken since—"

"We used one of Alyssa's pictures from her sixth-grade graduation last year and your last school picture, Hailey," said Donald. "I know you guys have changed since then, but people would've still recognized you."

"We slept in the car," Alyssa said. "So we didn't see any flyers."

"Well, we need to take them down," said Kathleen.

"What did the police do about this?" asked Hailey.

"They tried to find out about the kidnapper and how to get you guys back here," said Kathleen. "Sadly, they couldn't find him, so that was why we put flyers around town."

"So this man was a wizard?" asked Donald.

"Yep," said Alyssa.

"How did you defeat him?" asked Kathleen.

Alyssa told her without hesitating.

"Oh my god," said Donald. "Everything you did sounds so unsafe for children your ages."

"Well, at least we did it," said Alyssa.

"Still," said Kathleen.

"We're glad you're okay, though," said Donald

"Thanks." Alyssa smiled.

"So we were considering buying you guys some 'welcome back' gifts." Kathleen sat as the girls ate. "But maybe we should all go shopping together tomorrow."

"We're really tired, though," said Hailey.

"So after you eat, you can go to bed and unpack tomorrow," said Kathleen. "We can go shopping another time."

"Sounds cool," said Alyssa.

"Hey, where's my dad?" Hailey asked.

"He's sleeping," said Kathleen. "He'll actually be going to Happy Howard's Assisted Living Home next Tuesday."

"How's his memory?" asked Alyssa.

Kathleen sighed. "It comes and goes. He can figure out something for minutes, but then he forgets."

"Aw, that's terrible," said Alyssa.

"I'm going to miss him when he goes," said Hailey.

"I'm sure you will," said Kathleen. "Now before you go to bed, do you girls want some cookies?"

"Yeah," said Hailey.

"Sure," said Alyssa.

The girls each ate a cookie and then brought their stuff upstairs. Kathleen and Donald showed them the guest room where they'd sleep.

"Where's my dad sleeping?" asked Hailey.

"In the extra bedroom," responded Kathleen. "You want to say hi to him?"

Hailey nodded. Alyssa followed her and the grandparents into that room. Uncle Bruce slept in the bed, but Kathleen strode over to him and whispered to wake him up. He lifted himself up and opened his eyes.

"You two look familiar," he said. "What are your names?"

They told him.

"Right," he said.

Hailey and Alyssa walked over to him.

"We're going to miss you, Uncle Bruce," said Alyssa.

"Where am I going?" he asked.

"To a special home—where you can be happy," said Alyssa.

Hailey hugged him. "I love you."

"Bruce, wrap your arms around her too," said Donald.

"Oh." He hugged her back.

Alyssa did the same. Then she and Hailey walked into the guest room.

"It's so great to be back here," said Hailey.

"Yup," Alyssa said.

.

18

Nine days had passed since Alyssa and the other four had returned to New Jersey. Today was April third and Hailey and Alyssa had adjusted to the current time on Monday. Ever since, Kathleen and Donald had given them workbooks to do during the mornings. Because they still didn't have legal custody over Hailey, they couldn't obtain homeschooling licenses. In fact, Donald had said that he, Kathleen, and Hailey might move back to the old house either at the end of this month or the beginning of next month. That way, Hailey could return to school in Bursnell. They'd also taken down the missing-persons flyers.

Kathleen had just dropped Hailey off at her friend's house in Bursnell. She drove Alyssa to Bessie's Burger Shack, where Alyssa would meet with Jasmine and Madison for lunch. Alyssa sat in the front and listened to her iPod. Yesterday Kathleen and Donald had taken her and Hailey to the mall to buy cell phones and iPods. Because she loved hers so much, Alyssa had listened to every song until evening. She'd only bought twenty under Donald's iTunes account. She listened to the final song and noticed Bessie's Burger Shack outside her window. Kathleen turned into the lot and parked.

Stepping inside, Alyssa compared this place to a fast-food restaurant. People walked up to the counter to order their food, pay, and pick up their meals when the staff announced their order numbers. Kathleen and Alyssa purchased their lunch and waited while the chefs cooked.

The place had booth tables with cushioned seats, a polished floor, and a sign that said the burgers were cooked with fresh meat.

"Hi, Alyssa," Madison said.

Alyssa turned around. Madison walked with her mom.

"Hello." Alyssa waved.

"I'm coming to your birthday party, by the way," said Madison.

"Cool," said Alyssa.

"Are you guys waiting?" asked Mrs. Jennings.

"Yep," answered Alyssa.

Earlier in the week, Alyssa and the Flynns had checked out a restaurant in Bursnell called Cardinal Forest Diner to have Alyssa's birthday party. She also wanted to get her nails done after.

As Madison and her mom bought their food, a staff member called Kathleen and Alyssa's order number, and they picked up their meal. They selected a booth table and sat down. Alyssa watched the door open to reveal Jasmine and her mom.

Jasmine and Madison purchased their food and sat down. Kathleen and Mrs. Wilson left, but Mrs. Jennings stayed.

"Mom, don't you have to pick up Kaitlyn from karate?" asked Madison.

"She's not going to be done for about twenty minutes," said Mrs. Jennings. "Plus, home is out of the direction from Kaitlyn's karate class."

Alyssa swapped cell phone numbers with Madison and Jasmine. Jasmine's phone beeped, and she texted on it. She looked at Alyssa and Madison. "Did anyone listen to the news this morning?"

The two shook their heads.

"Well, my mom just did now," said Jasmine. "She said that last week, some scientists were on their way to this island in Fiji called Taveuni, and they stopped at Dermand on the way."

"And they announced it on the news today?" asked Madison.

"Yes," answered Jasmine.

"Why would they stop there?" Madison asked.

"Well—they saw Master Beau's and his workers' bodies," said Jasmine. "But they just described one as really heavy and the other three as thin. What's even scarier was that some white gas was rising out of Master Beau's body."

Alyssa clapped her hand over her mouth. "Could that be a ghost?"

"M-maybe," said Jasmine.

Alyssa sipped her Coke and thought about that "white gas" being a ghost. What if his spirit functioned like a living being? What if it wanted to find and kill her? Maybe she could figure out how to defeat it. Other methods besides the seashells Rosaline and Penelope had given her had to exist.

Alyssa finished her cheeseburger and fries and considered different ways to defeat Master Beau's possible spirit. But maybe it had no human functions at all. Maybe it'd just roam in random directions.

"Hey, Alyssa, what's your new house address?" asked Madison.

Alyssa said it.

"Can I also have your new home phone number?" Madison asked.

"Same here?" asked Jasmine.

Alyssa told them the number, and they programmed it into their phones.

"I wanted to invite you guys to my housewarming party tonight," Madison said to Jasmine and Alyssa.

"I'll come," said Alyssa.

"Me too," said Jasmine.

"Let's see if we can find more information about that gas," said Madison. "The party starts at six and ends at midnight."

Mrs. Jennings's phone made a texting sound, and she answered it.

"Madison, we need to go," said Mrs. Jennings. "Kaitlyn's karate class ended early."

"Why?" asked Madison.

"Some kid fell down and hurt his nose," said Mrs. Jennings. "He actually bled."

"Oh my god." Madison followed her mom outside.

Alyssa called Kathleen and told her to pick her up and if she could drive her to Madison's house for the event. She agreed to both.

*   *   *   *

That afternoon, Madison had also invited Alyssa to bring her family as well. Alyssa had told Hailey about the gas, but had also said that everything would be okay.

Donald drove onto Orion Street, and Alyssa looked out the window, seeing her and Hailey's old house. That brought Uncle Bruce into her mind, and she frowned about how he must feel in the assisted-living home since he'd moved in on Tuesday. She missed him and disliked the fact that she'd never see him again unless Kathleen and Donald could arrange a time to visit him. Even then, he may or may not recognize them.

The family parked outside of the Jennings' house on Draco Drive. Donald turned off the car and led everyone out. He rang the doorbell.

Mr. Jennings answered. "Hello."

The Flynns and Alyssa greeted him and stepped inside.

"Hey, Tara, have you seen Madison?" Mr. Jennings turned to Mrs. Jennings.

Mrs. Jennings poured potato chips into a bowl. "She must be looking for her cell phone."

"She can't find it?" asked Mr. Jennings.

"I'm not buying her another one." Mrs. Jennings shook her head.

"Mom, have you seen my dolls?" Kaitlyn ran into the kitchen.

"Now's not the time, Kaitlyn," said Mrs. Jennings.

Kaitlyn turned to Alyssa and the Flynns. "Hello."

"Hi, Alyssa!" Madison rushed down the stairs. She hugged her.

"Hey, Madison," said Alyssa.

"You're here kind of early," Madison said. "I don't even think it's six o'clock yet."

"It's actually five fifty-five," Alyssa stared into her phone.

"Well, do want to see if anything about that white—"

"Madison Christine Jennings, you are not doing that right now," said Mrs. Jennings.

"But, Mom, no one else is here yet," Madison said. "Plus, I promised Alyssa that I'd show her."

"You can call her tomorrow and talk about it with her privately," said Mrs. Jennings.

"Why can't I just tell her before anyone else comes?" asked Madison.

"Because I said so," said Mrs. Jennings.

"Madison, parties are supposed to be fun," Kaitlyn said. "You're literally being a party pooper."

"Shut up, Kaitlyn," muttered Madison.

The doorbell rang again, and Mr. Jennings answered it while Mrs. Jennings walked toward the counter. Alyssa turned around. Jasmine and her mom stood outside.

"Come on in." Mr. Jennings opened the door. "Janine, if you want to stay here, you're welcome to."

"I actually have to pick up my son from a friend's house," said Mrs. Wilson. "I'm sorry."

"It's okay," said Mr. Jennings. "Goodbye."

"Jasmine, I'm sorry, but I can't show you anything about the white gas," said Madison.

"Why not?" asked Jasmine.

"My mom won't let me," said Madison.

"We're not allowed to use the computer during parties," said Kaitlyn. "And Madison can't find her cell phone."

"Kaitlyn, stop telling them everything." Madison turned to Alyssa and Hailey. "You guys want some food or something?"

"Sure," said Alyssa.

They walked toward the kitchen, where various snacks and drinks rested on the counter. Alyssa helped herself to some Sprite, tortilla chips and salsa, fruit, and finger sandwiches. She sat at the table and ate but exhaled at what Mrs. Jennings had prohibited for Madison.

Whether the "ghost" could appear or disappear at will or not, it may still discover her. Maybe it wouldn't function. Still—Alyssa wanted to know its status as soon as possible.

After several people showed up, Alyssa, Jasmine, and Hailey threw their plates and cups away. Mr. and Mrs. Jennings mingled around and spoke to the guests. Kaitlyn walked with a girl around her age toward the basement.

"Guys, let's follow Kaitlyn," said Madison.

"Why are we doing that?" asked Jasmine.

"I'm going to turn on the TV and see if they talk about the white gas on the news," Madison said.

"Do you think they'll do it on a Saturday night?" asked Jasmine.

"I don't watch the news that much," said Madison. "So maybe."

The girls walked down the stairs and heard the TV. Kaitlyn and her friend watched *Phineas and Ferb* on the Disney Channel.

"How much longer is the episode?" Madison asked.

"I don't know," said Kaitlyn. "I just turned the TV on."

"So can we have a turn with it after *Phineas and Ferb* is over?" asked Madison.

"Can't you wait like Mom said?" asked Kaitlyn.

"I want to know now, though," said Madison.

"Too bad," said Kaitlyn.

Madison sighed and led Alyssa, Hailey, and Jasmine upstairs.

"Are any of our other friends coming?" asked Alyssa.

"No," said Madison. "They couldn't come."

"Who else did you invite?" asked Alyssa.

Madison listed the names.

"Madison?" Kaitlyn called from downstairs.

"Yeah?"

"You want to use *my* cell phone?" asked Kaitlyn.

"To look up more stuff about the white gas?" asked Madison.

"Yes. Go into my room."

"Why didn't you tell us earlier?" asked Madison.

"I don't know," said Kaitlyn. "I must've forgot or something."

"Let's go to Kaitlyn's room." Madison led Alyssa, Hailey, and Jasmine up to the second floor.

Kaitlyn's room had candy-pink walls, a daisy-shaped carpet, and Barbie dolls and stuffed animals all over the floor.

"Kaitlyn keeps forgetting to clean her room." Madison shut the door. She picked up Kaitlyn's cell phone.

Alyssa, Hailey, and Jasmine hovered over her to see what else shared information about the white gas from Master Beau's body.

"The white gas is soaring over the Pacific Ocean," said Jasmine. "It looks like a cloud close to the water."

"Do you know where it's going to go?" asked Hailey.

"Right now, it's near Hawaii," said Jasmine. "No one really knows what it is."

"It has to be Master Beau's spirit," said Alyssa.

"Well, it sounds like it's too simple to want to hurt you," said Hailey. "I think you'll be fine. Maybe it'll stay in Hawaii."

"Maybe." Alyssa shrugged. But her stomach compress. The gas might have taken the form of a cloud, but Alyssa couldn't find out if it would leave her alone. It could stay in Hawaii, or it may travel to the continental United States.

19

During the past two weeks, neither Madison nor Jasmine had contacted Alyssa about that white gas. They probably either hadn't kept up with the news or had heard nothing else about it.

Since Alyssa and Hailey had moved into Kathleen and Donald's house, they'd shared the bed in the guest room. Tossing and turning under the bed covers, Alyssa didn't touch or sense Hailey. That meant Hailey had woken up earlier. Alyssa lifted herself up and stretched. She turned to the digital clock and gasped at the time—ten-thirty. Her birthday party would start in two hours!

She jumped out of bed and did her morning bathroom routine. Then she peeled off her pale-green V-neck T-shirt and star-printed pajama pants and put on jeggings and a white square-neck shirt.

Not only had she become a teenager, but she could also obtain something Isabelle had promised to give her when she turned thirteen. But when—and how? Alyssa would spend some time at Cardinal Forest Diner. Then she'd go to Nails to Heaven. Nine other girls besides Madison and Jasmine would attend. Plus, it'd take a few minutes to drive there from the restaurant.

Alyssa entered the kitchen. Hailey, Kathleen, and Donald ate breakfast.

"Morning, guys," Alyssa said.

"Hey, it's the birthday girl," said Donald. "Come sit down and eat with us."

Alyssa sat and helped herself to a waffle, cereal, strawberries, and cranberry juice.

"Happy birthday, Alyssa," said Hailey.

"Thanks," said Alyssa.

"So you're thirteen years old now?" asked Kathleen.

Alyssa nodded.

"Wow, you're a teenager," said Kathleen.

"Uh huh," said Alyssa.

"And Hailey will become a teenager next July." Donald turned to Hailey. "One more year and a quarter of being a preteen."

Hailey nodded and ate her milk and cereal.

"Hey, when's Alex coming?" Alyssa asked.

"He called this morning to say that he was an hour away," said Donald.

"So he should be here soon," Kathleen said.

"Is he flying in?" asked Alyssa.

"Nope—he's driving," answered Donald.

"All the way from Ohio?" Alyssa asked.

"Yep," replied Donald. "He thought it'd be more convenient for you when you move in with him tomorrow."

"How?" asked Alyssa.

"Well, think about it," said Donald. "If you flew, your stuff wouldn't be at his house for several hours. Plus, you'd have to comply with the rules and restrictions at the airport."

"Oh—now I see," said Alyssa. "But I like road trips."

All her furniture had been left behind at her old house. However, at some point this evening, someone would pick up everything she'd left there and bring it here so that tomorrow it'd be ready to go into the moving van.

After breakfast, Alyssa headed toward the stairs—only to notice a car approaching her house. She turned to see a black Volvo turning into the driveway. That had to be Alex.

Alyssa grinned as she saw Alex stepping out. A goatee circled his mouth. His shoulder-length light-brown hair blew with the breeze. His opened black leather jacket bounced as he walked. Alyssa ran out to greet him. He formed a smile across his youthful face.

"Hey, Alex." Alyssa threw her arms around him.

"How are you, Alyssa?" Alex hugged her too.

"I'm good. It's great to see you."

"You too. Happy birthday."

"Thanks."

"All right, let me just get my stuff, and I'll meet up with you inside." Alex removed his hands from Alyssa. "Actually, you don't mind helping me carry some stuff, right?"

"Not at all."

Alex carried his duffel bag, and Alyssa carried his small backpack. The two went inside, where Hailey sat on a couch and read a *Discovery Girls* magazine.

"Hey, Hailey." Alex removed his black leather jacket.

Hailey looked up. "Hi."

"I don't know if you remember me." Alex grinned. "I'm Alyssa's godfather, Alex." He hung up his jacket and sat next to Alyssa and Hailey.

"Actually—I think I do now," said Hailey. "Weren't you the one who rushed into Alyssa's communion ten minutes late?"

Alex chuckled. "Yes, that was me."

Alyssa smiled but blushed too.

"So where are your grandparents, Hailey?" Alex asked.

"Upstairs," she answered.

"Hello." Kathleen jogged down the stairs with Donald. They greeted Alex.

"While we wait, do you want to open my present?" Alex asked Alyssa.

"Sure." Alyssa received the gift bag from him and pulled out a hot-pink glitter wallet. "Oh my god, this is adorable." She looked up at Alex. "Thank you."

"You're welcome." Alex smiled. "Why don't you read the card too?"

After Alyssa read it, Donald took everyone outside to go.

About twenty minutes had passed since everybody had left the house. During that time, thoughts of when Isabelle would come wandered into Alyssa's mind. What if the diner had no small spaces accessible to the customers? Also, that object she planned to give Alyssa had magic in it.

Wait—Isabelle had never said that she'd come during the day. Maybe she'd see Alyssa at night and meet her in the bathroom, like Simon had.

The group arrived at the restaurant and stepped inside the building, where a waiter led them into the private party room. Two tables had been set up—one for where Alyssa's friends sat and the other probably for her family. Madison and seven other girls sat together, and Alyssa joined them. They all wished her a happy birthday.

"Thanks, guys," she said.

She turned to the door as Jasmine and one of Hailey's friends walked inside. Jasmine sat across from her and Madison. After the last two of Alyssa's friends entered the room, a few waiters came inside to distribute baskets of bread and butter and take drink orders.

"So did either of you hear more about the white gas?" asked Alyssa.

"I don't have my phone with me," said Madison. "Otherwise, I'd look."

"What happened?" asked Alyssa.

"It'd died out by the time I found it, so now I have to charge it."

"I'll use my phone," said Jasmine.

"How come you guys haven't been keeping up with me about the white gas?" Alyssa asked.

"There hasn't been any news about it," Madison said.

"Really?" asked Alyssa.

"Nope," said Madison.

Jasmine looked into her phone. "Madison, maybe you didn't think it was too interesting that the cloud stayed in Hawaii for the past *two* weeks."

"Then how did it travel so far away in less than a week but stayed in Hawaii for two weeks?" asked Alyssa.

"I don't know," said Jasmine.

"Did it leave Hawaii yet?" asked Madison.

"I'm going to find that out now," said Jasmine.

The waiters came back with the drinks and cups of chicken-rice soup, salad plates, and bottles of different dressings. Jasmine put her phone away and helped herself to some salad. Alyssa and Madison did the same.

"Alyssa, who is that guy with the long hair?" Madison asked.

"My godfather." Alyssa revealed that she would move in with him tomorrow.

"I'm going to miss you," said Madison.

"Me too," said Jasmine.

Alyssa had her soup and salad until she heard a swish at the bottom of her feet. She leaned down and read the note.

Hi Alyssa,

First of all, happy birthday. Second, I need to meet you here to talk about Master Beau's spirit. I just appeared into a bathroom stall and am waiting for you in the ladies' room. Please come now.

Thank you,
Isabelle

Alyssa crumpled the note, shoved it into her jeggings pocket, and walked toward the door.

"Alyssa, where are you going?" Donald asked.

"Bathroom."

She continued her way out of the party area and walked to a waitress carrying drinks to ask her where the ladies' room was. She headed toward it and entered. But she saw no signs of Isabelle.

A stall opened, and guess who stepped out . . .

"Isabelle?" asked Alyssa.

"Mm-hm," she said. "I deliberately appeared in here and waited for you so that no one could see me."

"How?"

"Appearances inside ordinary places can automatically close doors."

"Oh, wow."

"Let's talk in the corner."

Alyssa followed her.

"Unfortunately, I don't have the object I was supposed to give you. But Mathias should give it to you tomorrow evening. Anyway, I want to talk to you about Master Beau's spirit."

"That *was* his spirit?"

Isabelle nodded.

"I knew it. How come it was able to go to Hawaii in less than a week but—"

"There was a wizarding battle on one of the islands, and some of the magic coming from the wands affected the atmosphere."

Alyssa dropped her jaw. "How?"

"It made it really hot, like, high into the triple digits. And some of the magic made it last for two weeks. Spirits can't travel in temperatures more than a hundred- and five-degrees Fahrenheit."

"Why not?"

"It has to do with the air in the spirit. For some reason, it can't handle extremely hot temperatures. But now his spirit has left Hawaii and on its way to the continental United States."

Alyssa gasped.

"I hate to scare you more, but it's going to travel to wherever you live."

"I'm moving to Ohio tomorrow,"

"Then that's where it'll go. But there's no need to worry. It can't hurt you for at least six months."

"What's going to happen then?"

"There's some magic liquid that can turn spirits into living forms. It takes at least six months to make."

"What is it?"

"I don't know. But it's new and still not tested."

"At least I'll get that object tomorrow." Alyssa paused. "Wait— I thought wizards weren't allowed to travel with magical objects."

"Mathias obtained a license for it."

"I didn't know you could do that."

"It just went into effect last week. You have to be eighteen, though."

"Oh."

"Well, I'm going to go now. Happy birthday."

"Thanks."

Isabelle stepped into a bathroom stall. Alyssa left and headed back into the party section, where waiters now served the entrées. Plates of burgers, chicken tenders, quesadillas, fried chicken, and roast turkey with gravy rested in the center of the tables. The staff also brought out plates of french fries, onion rings, mashed potatoes, coleslaw, corn, and mixed vegetables. The guests served themselves and ate.

"Why were you in the bathroom for so long?" Madison asked. Alyssa told her.

"Isabelle was here?" whispered Madison.

"She told me she was going to be here," said Alyssa. "She said it right before we left Yanowic."

"What did she give you?" asked Jasmine.

Alyssa explained that she didn't have it and that Mathias would give it to her tomorrow evening. "I found out more about that gas."

"What is it?" asked Madison.

Alyssa whispered it in her ear.

"Oh my god," said Madison. "Th-that's scary."

"What happened?" asked Jasmine.

Alyssa told her.

Jasmine brightened her eyes. "That *is* scary."

"Yeah," Alyssa said. "But I think I'll find a way to defeat it." She turned to the other girls. None of them paid attention.

"Did Isabelle say what you needed?" asked Jasmine.

Alyssa shook her head. "But that's okay. Maybe I'll have her as a mentor again. Even if I don't—I'm sure there will be someone to help me."

"Magic doesn't scare you anymore?" asked Madison.

"Nope," said Alyssa. "I actually need to tell my godfather about it at some point."

"You think he'll believe you?" Jasmine asked.

"I already told him before I got kidnapped," Alyssa said.

"Oh," said Jasmine.

Alyssa continued to eat.

Lunch lasted for about a half hour, and then the waiters took the plates back. Alyssa told Madison and Jasmine that she'd be safe for at least six months. But the two still worried.

Jasmine breathed. "I hope you're okay, Alyssa."

"Me too," she said.

A waitress arrived, holding a whipped-cream-iced cake with lit candles. She headed toward Alyssa. "Okay, make a wish." She placed the cake down in front of her.

Alyssa looked up, smiling as everyone at her table looked at her.

"Come on, Alyssa." Madison smiled.

"Okay, okay," she rushed out of her mouth. "I . . . I'm—"

"You don't want us to keep staring at you?" asked one of her other friends.

"No," giggled Alyssa.

"Shut your eyes," said Hailey from her table. "Pretend no one's here."

"Okay." Alyssa shut her eyes and blew out the candles.

Everybody applauded, and the waitress took the cake back to cut it.

A few minutes later, the same waiters as before carried small plates of cake slices. Alyssa received her piece and took a bite, tasting the fluffiness of the vanilla flavor and the chocolate buttercream filled inside. She ate until nothing except crumbs remained on her plate. Then baskets of fruit and assorted cookies arrived. Alyssa took a few kinds of each.

"Alyssa, you're really going to eat all that?" asked Hailey from the other table.

"Yeah," said Alyssa.

"Don't worry," said Alex. "It's your birthday. Eat as much as you'd like."

"Thank you." Alyssa ate until her stomach filled up.

Everyone chatted for about ten more minutes until Kathleen and Donald paid the check. The group headed out of the restaurant so that the girls would have their nails painted. Tonight Alyssa would pack. She hoped that Mathias would not meet her in public like Isabelle.

20

Last night, after everyone had packed up her furniture, Alyssa had occupied the basement. Alex had taken the extra room.

Alyssa's digital clock alarm went off. She jumped out of her bed and turned it off. The time was six-thirty a.m. Alex wanted to leave at seven so that he could arrive at his house sooner. Despite that, Alyssa crawled back under her bed covers and fell back asleep but the light switch came on. She lifted herself up, watching Alex step down the stairs, already dressed in his day clothes.

"Alyssa, it's time to get ready," he said. "The moving van's already here."

"Okay." Alyssa slid off her bed.

"Are you all packed up?" asked Alex.

Alyssa nodded.

"All right. I'll let you get ready." He headed back up the stairs.

Alyssa peeled off her long-sleeved pink shirt and striped pajama pants and put on jeans, a tank top, and plaid shirt. She did her morning bathroom routine and took her suitcase upstairs.

"Sweetheart, do you want me to help you take more things upstairs?" Alex asked.

"Sure," said Alyssa.

She and Alex headed back to the basement to grab more bags of birthday presents, extra clothes, and anything else that couldn't fit in her suitcase.

"Can we go down now?" asked one of the moving van men as Alyssa and Alex stepped back onto the ground floor.

"Um . . ." Alex turned to Alyssa.

"Go ahead," she said.

As the workers took her furniture upstairs, Kathleen, Donald, and Hailey entered the basement, still in their pajamas.

"I'm going to miss you, Alyssa." Hailey hugged her.

"Me too," she said.

The two let go.

"Don't forget to call or e-mail me," said Hailey.

"Sure," said Alyssa.

"Same here," said Donald. "You have a good trip, kiddo."

"Thanks," Alyssa said. "I'll keep in touch with all of you."

She went outside and settled into the front seat of Alex's car since he had invited her there. Then he drove off.

"Did you put this blanket and pillow here?" asked Alyssa.

"Uh huh," said Alex. "I wanted to make you comfortable."

"Cool. Thanks."

"I still can't believe what happened to you."

Yesterday, after the party had ended and all the girls had gotten their nails done, he'd told her about Hailey, Kathleen, and Donald discussing everything they'd known about her and Hailey when they'd been kidnapped.

"I know—it was scary," Alyssa said.

"Hailey even told me about some 'white gas.'"

"I know what that is."

"You do?"

"Uh huh. It's the evil wizard's ghost."

Alex gasped. "Oh my god."

"But on the bright side, nothing will happen for at least six months."

"W-what if something does?"

"Then we'll find a way to resolve it." Alyssa yawned, covering her mouth.

"There really are such ways?"

"There were ways to resolve other kinds of magic. But can we talk about that later?"

"Why?"

"I'm tired."

"All right, go ahead and sleep. I'll wake you up when we stop for lunch."

"Okay." Alyssa leaned back on the seat's pillow, put her blanket on, and dozed off.

About five and a half hours had passed since Alyssa and Alex had left Kathleen and Donald's house. The two had finished lunch at Panera Bread and walked back to the car. During that time, Alex had told Alyssa that when he had attended college, he'd forget a lot of requests and belongings when it came to social situations. Then he'd mentioned that'd been how he and Alyssa's mom had broken up when he was eighteen and she was twenty-three.

"What exactly happened?" Alyssa asked as Alex pulled out of the parking slot.

"She gave me her wallet so that I could go buy myself some lunch."

"You couldn't do it yourself?"

"She was commuting to school, and I was living in the dorms. I had run low on cash, and my debit card had problems. But it was close to spring break, so I did get more money after."

"Oh. So why was my mom still in college when she was supposed to graduate the year before?"

"She started college a year late. Anyway, I accidentally left the wallet behind. When your mom and I came back—it was gone."

"Oh no."

"She actually dumped me for that."

"So you weren't invited to my parents' wedding or—"

"Nope. She also didn't invite me to your first baptism or even dare to call me."

"Wow."

"I didn't bother to call her either. But I did get another girlfriend later."

"When?"

"Around the time you were born, which was five years after your mom dumped me. But I only dated her for four and a half years."

"What happened after that?"

Alex sighed. "She died from a snake bite."

"Aw, I'm sorry."

"It's okay. I was so sad, though, and couldn't find any other women to date. So I called your mom and talked to her."

"You still had her phone number?"

"Yup."

"What did she say?"

"She was actually really nice. And she felt bad for never talking to me, so she invited me to be your godfather and designated me as the legal guardian in the event that something happened to them."

Alyssa nodded.

"She reconnected with me and introduced me to you father."

"Yeah, I remember."

"No, this was over the phone a few months before I first met you."

"Oh." Alyssa formed a weak grin.

Because of traffic, Alex and Alyssa hadn't left Pennsylvania until now. Only a few minutes after five had passed, and Alyssa's stomach moaned. But she saw no restaurants outside. Just woodlands and hills surrounded the street.

"Sweetie, are you hungry?" Alex asked.

"Uh huh."

"So am I. Since it's your birthday, you get to pick what kind of food you're interested in."

"Uh . . . how about steak?"

"Sounds good to me."

Once they reached a town, Alyssa looked around for places that would probably serve steak. She saw a small diner, various shops, strip malls, fast-food restaurants, and a pottery studio. But a sign for Virgo's Steakhouse stood a few hundred feet away.

"Alex, can we go to Virgo's Steakhouse?"

"Okay." Alex pulled into the parking lot.

The two stepped inside, and Alyssa looked around at the scarlet-and-beige color scheme. Candles stood at each table. Pictures covered every other space on the wall. A waiter sat Alyssa and Alex at a small table and gave them menus. The two ordered their food and drinks. A few minutes later, the waiter gave them their drinks.

"So, Alyssa, I just want to tell you how things are going to work at my house."

"Okay."

"The first week, you can relax and get used to my house. But after that, I have some rules."

Alex told Alyssa what guidelines would apply to her at his place. There would be no leaving dishes in the sink; they must go straight into the dishwasher after being rinsed. Alex had a dog as well, so Alyssa had to help take care of it. She also had to make her bed when she had no school. When school started again, Alyssa couldn't watch TV until she completed all her homework, and she was forbidden to view any if she had a quiz or test within the next two days.

Alyssa didn't mind those. But Alex mentioned that although he'd have a cleaning lady come to his house since he didn't want Alyssa home alone all day while he'd worked, she had to do her own laundry after this week.

"Can I play music while I do my laundry?" asked Alyssa.

"Of course." Alex smiled.

The waiter returned with the food. Alyssa ate her steak, and Mathias came to her mind. Right. He would see her tonight. But how would Alex react to his presence? Maybe he'd freak out—or he'd welcome Mathias after finding out that he had mentored Alyssa in Fiji.

However, Alyssa still hoped that Mathias would meet her in private. She'd also have to hide the object so that other people wouldn't find it. But she didn't own a safe. She had kept her money in plastic Ziploc bags and in her closet. So she would have to resolve the issue when she arrived at Alex's house.

"Alyssa, there's an ice cream parlor across the street," Alex said. "Do you want to go there?"

"Sure."

"It'll also be a birthday gift, by the way."

After finishing, Alex and Alyssa walked across the street since there was no sign enforcing tow-away actions if a person left the property.

The two entered, and Alyssa read the ice cream flavors, creations, and toppings on the menu above her. Besides the classic vanilla, chocolate, and strawberry flavors, others included cake batter, cotton candy, mocha chip, and blueberry. Alyssa picked cake batter with cocoa-cookie crumbs, chocolate syrup, and whipped cream.

She ate, but a swish occurred under her feet. Alex had gone to the bathroom about a minute ago, so Alyssa assumed that he would come out in a minute. She picked up the paper and read it.

Hi Alyssa,

Right now, Isabelle and I are eating dinner, and I should be at your new home as soon as you get there. I'm not only giving you the object Isabelle had told you about but also something else. If you don't have a safe, that's fine. An old shoebox will do.

Thank you,
Mathias

Alyssa crumpled the note and threw it away. Walking back to her table, she saw Alex exit the men's room.

"Are you ready to go, Alyssa?"

"Yep."

Despite the darkness that had filled the sky, Alyssa still saw the rustic scenery surrounding her. Trees made up forests, and hills sloped. Sheep, cattle, and horses meandered on the farms. Fields and meadows spread up to several acres.

Alex and Alyssa passed a few towns before they turned onto a street called Delphinius Street, which led them to Gemini Road. Each house had a large yard with trees; some even had gates.

Alex pulled into a house without a gate, but trees blocked some of the home's view. The house light revealed what the building looked like. It had light-green trims with a porch and balcony. The garage stood next to the house.

"Welcome to your new home, Alyssa." Alex turned off the car.

Alyssa hopped out and took her bags. During the ride, the moving-van people had called Alex and had said that everything had already arrived. Alex had also called his neighbor a half hour ago to tell her that she could go home since he'd arrive in time for his dog.

Approaching the front door, Alyssa heard barking. Alex unlocked the door, opened it, and turned on the lights. A yellow Labrador retriever trotted toward him, panting. Then it sniffed Alyssa, and she petted.

"What's your dog's name?" asked Alyssa.

"Scooter," answered Alex.

Scooter ran into the kitchen.

"So, Alyssa, do you want a tour of the house, or are you too tired?"

"I'm exhausted."

"That's fine. I'll give you a tour tomorrow."

"Okay. Hey, when do I start school?"

"The end of this month. Not tomorrow but next Monday."

Alyssa nodded.

"Would you like me to carry your suitcase to your new room?"

"Sure."

"It actually used to be the guest room. But now I moved everything downstairs."

Alyssa giggled, thinking about how Kathleen and Donald had done the exact thing. She carried her backpack and purse while Alex took her suitcase. She then grabbed everything else she owned and went to her room. Her bed, dresser, and everything else in the moving truck had come. The bed leaned against the wall on her right side, but the dresser and desk stood in opposite places.

Alyssa shrugged. "Hey, when did you move everything from this room downstairs?"

"Shortly before coming to Hailey's grandparents' house," said Alex. "All right, sweetheart, I'm going to go do some work. You can just relax and unpack tomorrow."

"Okay."

Alex left and shut the door.

Then a swish sounded. Mathias had arrived. "Hello."

"Hi, Mathias," said Alyssa. "Is everything you told me about in the bag?"

"Uh huh. Hey, can you lock the door so that in case someone comes, they don't see me?"

Alyssa nodded and did so.

Mathias pulled out an old shoebox and a duct tape roll. He took out a small dome with a silver lump in the center. "This is a warning dome. When nothing dangerous is going on, blue air will spread inside. But when something dangerous is coming, the light will be bright orange."

"Okay."

Mathias reached into his bag and brought out what looked like a glow stick that kids sometimes used at dance parties. "This is a magic light stick. It turns danger away when it approaches your house."

"How?"

"It blocks out any evil sorcerers or creatures like a shield."

"So they'll be unable to come into my house?"

"Yep. But it only works on what I mention. It won't work on ordinary people or dark magic from wands or potions."

Alyssa nodded.

"Keep these things safe and hidden from other people. Do not show them to anyone except whoever you're living with, unless there's dark magic going on."

Alyssa nodded as Mathias handed her the objects. The dome turned blue, and she smiled.

"Put them away now."

Alyssa placed them in the shoebox and shut it with tape. Mathias then disappeared.

Alyssa put the box in her closet, behind some old stuff, and closed it. Hopefully, the next six or more months would stay free of danger and dark wizardry.

About the Author

Sunayna Prasad has published a few books between her late teens and her mid-twenties. She has won a Pacific Book Review Award for her novel, *Wizardry Goes Wild*, which will return as a new edition, like *The Frights of Fiji,* formerly *From Frights to Flaws*. The sequel is now titled *The Unruly Curse*. Sunayna also has a blog on different creative and entertaining topics, including writing and fiction. It is called "Sunayna Prasad's Blog".

Aside from writing, Sunayna also likes to cook, do art, and watch videos online. She has graduated from college in May 2017 and is looking to continue more writing as well as hold a coding job soon. Sunayna lives on Long Island, NY.

Made in the USA
Monee, IL
06 March 2020